THE PLAYBOY

J. S. COOPER

BLURB

A-list actor and former rock star Oracle Lion, also known as Zach Houston, needs no introduction. He's the handsome playboy of Hollywood, and women around the world want to be with him. Every woman, it seems, except for Piper Meadows. Piper wants nothing to do with a man like Oracle. And that's why she pretends she has no idea who he is when she first meets him. She doesn't know this will make Oracle see her as a challenge. She doesn't know that her lack of interest will lead to an offer of friendship that she'll find hard to refuse.

Piper Meadows thinks she knows what a man like Oracle Lion wants. She thinks she knows what a real playboy is like, but Oracle confounds all of those ideas. For, while Oracle is a playboy, he's so much more than that. As their friendship grows more confusing, neither one of them is prepared for what happens next. As they get to know each other, they find themselves caught up in a web of hot passion, lies, and love. Then comes an explosion of secrets that are going to rock both of their worlds. They have no idea that both of their lives are about to be turned upside down.

❀ Created with Vellum

DEDICATION

This book is for any woman that has fantasized about dating a movie star. Sometimes dreams do come true.

PROLOGUE

YOU KNOW A MAN WILL BE GOOD IN BED IF HE CAN DANCE. There's something about the way a man can move back and forth while holding the small of your back that alerts you to the fact that he can multitask. When a man knows how to both turn you on and move you effortlessly across the room, you know you have a winner.

That's just my theory, of course. I'm not exactly an expert at men. I'm still single. Still bouncing around between emotionally unavailable men, cocky bastards, and cheap asses who like to make you think you're lucky to be spending your money on them. Yeah, no thanks. I'll keep my hundred dollars to myself and have some fun at Sephora, shopping for overpriced makeup to make myself look beautiful for the next man who's going to attempt to show me a good time.

I'm not jaded. I do believe he exists, somewhere out there, stuck between Mars and an ever-expanding Venus. I should have known, though, that the man who'd finally sweep me off of my feet wasn't going to be the regular sort of Prince Charming.

And that's what I'm here to preach to the world. (Don't

worry, I'm not going to jump onto a pulpit and quote verses from the Bible; I'd be laughed out of church or banished. Somehow, I don't think the reverend would be happy to hear me to talk about my tongue test ... but I digress). I'm here to say that sometimes the man who sweeps you off your feet is not the man you think he's going to be. Sometimes the man who turns your world upside down can also turn it right side up—though why he's turning it upside down in the first place is anyone's guess.

Now, this next one might shock you, but sometimes the man you hate with a passion is the man that you will love with a passion. Trust me, I never believed it either.

Until it happened.

Look, I've always wanted to be in love. I've always dreamed of the moment the man of my dreams would sweep me up into his arms and never let me go. I just had no idea that the man that was to take my breath away would be *him*.

CHAPTER 1

ORACLE

"I'll have a red velvet ... no, wait, a lemon drop ... no wait —a mint chocolate cupcake." The woman in front of me giggled slightly as she threw her hands up in the air. "You know what, I'll take all three of them, sorry." She turned around slightly and gave me a sweet smile. "Sorry about that, I'm having a horrible time deciding what I want today." There was an earnest expression in her brown eyes.

I shrugged as she played around with her hair. "No worries," I said, my voice deeper than usual. I felt like a bit of an idiot in my LA Dodgers baseball cap and huge dark aviators. I also had a fake mustache on my face, and I was wearing an old red and white plaid shirt. I knew looked like some sort of hillbilly just come to town from North Dakota, but I didn't care. It was better than being recognized and accosted by every wannabe actor in town.

And seeing as I lived in Los Angeles, that meant I was avoiding a tremendous amount of people.

"Let me buy your cupcakes." The lady turned back to me

again with an impish smile. "I was reading an article yesterday about this Starbucks in Seattle that has had the pay-it-forward coffee movement going for two weeks straight." She kept babbling on while I just stared at her without a word. I had no idea what she was talking about. "So, what do you want?"

"What do I want?" I repeated her words and looked her over. She was pretty, in that fresh-from-the-farm sort of way. She had no makeup on, but her face was fresh and clean, with naturally glowing pink cheeks. Her lips looked like they had a touch of lip gloss and her unruly black hair cascaded down her back. She stood in front of me in a pair of tight blue jeans and a plain white T-shirt that clung delightfully to her curves. If I'd been a different sort of guy, I might have tried to chat her up, but I wasn't.

"Yeah, what sort of cupcake do you want? Or do you want multiple cupcakes? It's so hard to choose, isn't it?"

"I'm getting a dozen, so I think I'll pay for myself, but thanks." I nodded to let her know that the conversation was over, but she didn't seem to get the hint.

"Wow, a dozen. Lucky ducky! Are you having a party?" She looked at me again and I could see her taking in my full appearance. I wondered what she thought as she stared at me. There was no way she knew she was standing in front of Oracle Lion. No way she knew she was chatting with Hollywood royalty.

"No party. I'm going to eat them all myself," I lied, and she just looked at me with wide eyes, processing what I'd said. "I live on cupcakes, you see, I don't eat anything else."

"You what?" Her jaw dropped, and I started laughing at her expression.

"You shouldn't be so gullible, lady." I started to take my sunglasses off so that we could make actual eye contact, but then I remembered I had on a disguise. "Of course, I don't just eat cupcakes."

"Funny." She grinned, not seeming to be annoyed that I'd called her gullible. I liked that she didn't take herself too seriously. It was refreshing to meet a woman who didn't overreact to every comment I made. "Are you a comedian?"

"Yeah, I'm Chris Rock. I just changed skin colors in the bathroom, you know how it goes."

"Changed skin colors?" She just shook her head as she smiled. "Really?"

"Well, he's black and I'm white, so you would have thought something was off if I hadn't mentioned it."

"Yeah, but I think the biggest thing that's off is that he's funny and you're not." She laughed. "Oh, LA," she said to herself and I didn't have to ask her what she meant. Los Angeles was full of weirdos, otherwise known as unique personalities, and she most probably had me lumped into that group.

"I'm not a racist, by the way. I know you may think that because of my bad joke."

"Don't worry, I don't think you're a racist. I don't think you're funny either, but still not a racist."

"What's your name?" I asked her curiously. She had a nice smile and, well, the longer I stared at her body, the more I realized that she was a sexy bombshell as well.

"Piper. You?"

"Uh, Jimbo," I said the first name that came to mind. "Jimbo Clampett." I held my hand out. "Nice to make your acquaintance, ma'am."

"Jimbo Clampett?" She didn't sound convinced, but she didn't question me. "So, are you sure I can't buy you a cupcake, Jimbo?"

"Jethro," I said what I was thinking out loud and I saw her small smile turn to a frown for a second.

"Sorry, what?" It was her turn to be confused.

"Jimbo Jethro." I nearly drawled the name but knew that would be too much. I was playing a role now, and while I didn't know this woman from Adam, I was drawn to our weird conversation. "I'm Jimbo Jethro, and I'm from North Dakota."

"Really, now?" Her mouth curled up at the side, and I watched as she shook her head slightly. "Jimbo Jethro Clampett from North Dakota, huh?" She grinned. "Do you live in Beverly Hills as well?"

"Why, no, ma'am," I said.

It was then that I noticed that the shop assistant was staring at us both, a bemused expression on her face. I could see her looking at my attire for a few seconds and then her expression changed. Her face grew still and I could tell that she was trying to imagine me without the glasses and cap. She was a local and probably dealt with a lot of stars in odd costumes coming in to buy their world-renowned cupcakes. Well, the stars with no personal assistants. Maybe I really did need to invest in one.

"You're funny, you know that?" Piper grinned at me and then laughed, a long, slow, delicious laugh that made me want to laugh as well. Piper's enthusiasm for life was contagious, and a part of me wondered how she would act if she knew who I was. "You're not Chris Rock, but you're funny."

"Thanks," I said and then because I couldn't stop myself, "and you're pretty funny yourself. Cute, too."

"Well, I do my best."

She started playing with her hair again and I wanted to reach over and pull on one of her corkscrew curls. She was more than cute. She was beautiful in that completely unaware way. And her body was dynamite. I could only imagine the sorts of fun that we could have if I took her back to my place. I could imagine, but of course, I wouldn't do it. No matter how much I wanted to. And then she started nibbling on her lower lip and playing with her hair at the same time as she noticed the tub of banana pudding. I could see her debating in her head whether or not she should get some.

"Got a craving, huh?" I whispered into her ear as I took a step toward her. My whisper must have startled her because she jumped back into me as my breath tickled her ear. I can't lie, I was hoping for that response.

"Oh, well, you know." She looked nervous now and I could see her eyes darting to my lips. Lips that were now quite close to hers. "I love banana pudding, but I'm already getting cupcakes, and Alexa will be a little upset if I bring too many sweets back. She tries to avoid sugar, you see."

"I see," I said, not caring about Alexa or her dislike of sugar. "You should get what you want. Life is too short to not be happy. Shoot, if you want banana pudding and cupcakes and ice cream and whipped cream, you should get it. Especially the whipped cream." I stared at her to see if she made the connection in my reference to whipped cream, but it seemed to go over her head. Poor girl was probably too innocent for a man like me.

"Yes, true."

"I like to go after what I want," I said, and I watched as she licked her lips. "Are you the same?"

"I, uh, I ..." She tripped over her words, and I was about to go in for the kill, when I saw my buddy Jackson headed toward the door. If he walked in, I knew he would be recognized, and I knew he would out me. I didn't want that. I didn't want Piper's expression changing to one of excitement that she was talking to a Hollywood star. I didn't want our whole innocent interaction tainted. It had been fun, and it had been the first time I felt I'd been up to let my guard down in a while.

"I've got to run, hon, but have a good day," I said quickly

then made a beeline for the door to make sure that Jackson didn't make it inside first. I could see the look of disappointment on her face, and I felt a hardening in my groin that told me that she wasn't the only one upset that I'd had to leave. It had been for the best, though. There was no way she would have wanted to eat a shit-ton of cupcakes around me if she'd known who I really was.

For some reason, women didn't tend to eat much around me at all.

I SAT ON THE COUCH, cupcake-less, and thought about Piper, the hottie in the cupcake store. She'd been fun, but there was no point thinking about her or what could have been; the moment was gone. I was curious how she would have reacted if she'd known who I really was. Would she have gushed all over me, hoping to be my playmate for the evening?

I made my way through the gossip websites to see if I was mentioned, and then stopped when I saw my name on the top of one of the pages.

"Hollywood Heartthrob Oracle Lion dumps another model," read the top headline on a national news website. I clicked on the article and saw a photo of Cassie Cash and me on the beach in Kauai, Hawaii, and skimmed the first paragraph. I couldn't stop myself from laughing at the words that the reporter had used to describe my relationship with Cassie. "Hot and heavy since they met in London"? "Late nights spent skinny dipping"? Complete and utter fabrications. I didn't even know Cassie that well. We'd both been hired by a top designer to do a photoshoot for a new summer wear line, and while we'd flirted on the beach and gone to dinner one night, that had been it. She was a hottie, but I hadn't even tried to kiss her; she'd been too ditzy and plastic, even for me.

I shut down my laptop without bothering to read the rest of the article. It didn't matter to me. In fact, it was great for my image to be in the news all the time. I didn't care if it was for my movies or my women. I knew I'd have to call my mom, though; even after all these years, she still believed all the trash gossip these wannabe reporters wrote about me. And she still got upset. I sighed at the thought of having to explain to her once again that no, I hadn't just dumped another model, and no, I wasn't dating anyone special and no, I was not planning on getting married and having kids any time soon. I didn't plan on it ever, but I knew she didn't want to hear that.

"Yo, Oracle, Bruno says there are three chicks at the door. He wants to know if he should let them in?"

My best friend Jackson Camden walked into my study looking up from his cell phone with a quizzical look. I shook my head. Bruno was Jackson's personal bodyguard and was always around. He was a cool guy, but he took his job way too seriously. Though I suppose that his job as the bodyguard of one of the most famous rock stars in the world was pretty important.

"Nah, they aren't with me." I shook my head. "Most probably some groupies or reporters."

"Pity." He grinned. "Would have been nice to get the party started right tonight." He winked at me, and I groaned. "What? You know you want to have fun tonight as well."

"It's not like when we were in college, dude. We can't just hook up with randoms." I laughed as we walked through the doorway down the hall to my kitchen. "Paparazzi will be there, ready and waiting."

"Pity." Jackson chuckled to himself and pulled out two

beers from my fridge. "Dude, you have nothing but beer in here."

"Yeah, I know. Rosa needs to go shopping. She's been on vacation with her family." I shrugged as I caught the IPA he'd thrown me. "She's back next week."

Rosa was my housekeeper, and she basically kept my place clean and stocked. Without her, I wouldn't know what to do. I'd have dirty towels and no food, ever. Though I'm pretty sure my mom would love for me to fire Rosa so she could come on over and take care of everything. There was no way in hell that I was going to let that happen, though. I liked my independence way too much.

"You're spoiled, you know that, right, Zach?" Jackson used my real name as he chugged on his beer. "I'm hungry."

"Then order a pizza or something." I rolled my eyes. "I'm not here to feed you. You can do it yourself." We walked back down the hall into my den, and he sat on the black leather couch while I sat on the large red concrete chair shaped like the palm of a hand. My interior decorator had said would be a great statement piece in my house. She'd been correct; it stood out in the plain room, but not in a good way. I thought the chair was ugly and uncomfortable, but then again, it went with the house. I'd bought it about a year ago, but it had never really felt like a home.

"So, what are we doing tonight? We gotta have fun. I'm flying out tomorrow."

"You're leaving tomorrow?" I adjusted myself on the hard surface and stared at his spiked black hair and all-black leather outfit. "I thought you were here for a month?"

"Nah, going back to New York tomorrow evening. Going to be on *The Today Show* on Monday." He shrugged as if it was no big deal, which, of course, it wasn't. We'd both been on TV more times than we could count. To be honest, it was boring to be on TV now. Almost everything about being rich and famous was boring. "So where are we going? Brad was telling me about some cool new club in We-Ho that I thought we could check out. Meet a couple of ladies, have them begging to be with us."

"Begging to be with us?" I scoffed and then laughed. It wasn't like his words weren't true. Every woman wanted to be with Jackson Camden and Oracle Lion, the so-called foxes of Hollywood. I was used to it by now. "Sounds cool. Haven't hooked up in a while."

"What's it been? A week?" Jackson asked with a raised eyebrow and we both laughed. "So, how's the new movie going? Started shooting yet?"

"No, they just changed directors." I shook my head. "Who knows what's going to happen next. I'm looking at some scripts myself, going to try my hand at directing or something like that."

"Yeah?" He nodded and took another chug. "Finally. You've been saying that since college."

"I know."

I looked at the original 1941 poster of *Citizen Kane* hanging on my wall. At the top of the poster, it said, "Everybody's Talking About It! It's Terrific," and next to the words was an image of Orson Welles. *Citizen Kane* had been the movie that had changed my life as a kid. I could still remember watching it with my mom. She had always loved the old movies and I loved sharing them with her. I'd been mesmerized by the screen, the black-and-white images and Orson Welles. He hadn't been a particularly handsome man, but he captured your attention and never let it go.

Ever since I'd seen that movie, I'd wanted to make movies. Real, hardcore, deep, thought-provoking movies. Movies that made people talk about issues, movies that made people talk about me. I'd achieved one of the two, but the movies I made now were empty and tasteless. I wanted some-

J. S. COOPER

thing different in my life. I looked around the large room at the obscene paintings and sculptures that made people talk. The bright red accent wall that offended my vision every time I sat in here. Everything about my life was fake and for show and in a way shallow.

"So, you're going to direct *Babymaker Four*, then?" Jackson laughed so hard at his joke that he tipped forward. His eyes met mine with an expression of mirth and I just smiled at him in response. Jackson knew how much I hated the *Babymaker* movies, but they were what was responsible for my substantial bank account. America loved me as the baby-maker, and while the movies had catapulted my career, he knew I wasn't happy.

"Sorry, dude. I know it's not funny." He sighed and sat back, his eyes suddenly looking sad. "Who would have thought this would be where we'd end up, eh?"

All of the life seemed to have been sucked out of him at that moment. We were only thirty-five, but both of us were disillusioned with life and our respective careers. When we'd enrolled as freshmen at the University of Central Florida and formed a student band, we'd never dreamed that we'd make it this big. Never in our wildest dreams had we thought that we'd be A-list stars with the world at our feet.

Only we didn't really have the world at our feet.

"Funny." I shook my head and sighed. "No, I'm not going to be making bloody *Babymaker Four*."

"I thought I saw on *Access Hollywood* that you signed a thirty-million-dollar deal and you're starring with Frenchie?" He tilted his head to the side. "Did they get it wrong?"

"No." My voice was abrupt as I stood up. "I don't wanna talk about it. Wanna hit up Chateau Marmont for dinner? My treat."

"Your treat?" Jackson laughed. "As if. I'm your guest, I got it."

12

"Are you really my guest if I never invited you?" I raised an eyebrow at him and we both laughed. Jackson walked over to me and swung an arm around my back.

"I've missed you, brother," he said as he patted my shoulders. "It's been too long."

"Well, who told you to go and be an international rock star?"

"You could always join the band again. We could go on tour together."

"Nah, those days are past me. You know I only did the music for fun."

"I know, I know. Your heart is with the movies."

"Yeah, something like that." I nodded. "Okay, I'm off to shower and get changed. You know where your room is. Feel free to use any of the five other bathrooms on offer."

"Cool. Also, just want to check that ..." His voice trailed off as I held my hand up with a chuckle.

"Yes, Jackson. Feel free to bring back any chicks tonight, but just make sure they're gone by the morning, please. I don't need a repeat of what happened last time."

"Got it, got it." He grinned. "And hey, I didn't know that one of the girls stayed. I honestly thought that all of them had gone. I counted five heads leaving after our quickie in the shower."

"Yeah, you counted five heads, but you had six women over." I tried not to roll my eyes. "I really don't know how you do it."

"I don't remember you being so sanctimonious that night. Didn't you have a threesome with those two waitresses?"

"Perhaps." I laughed. "Just make sure they're all gone in the morning."

"Yes, sir." He saluted me like I was some sort of captain. "Here's to making sure my harem is all gone in the morning."

"Yeah, please make sure. I'm going to the beach shack

tomorrow night after you leave, so don't want any unwelcome guests staying over."

"You ever going to let me see that place?" Jackson asked, and I just laughed without answering.

He knew the answer to that. The beach shack was my private domain. The only person that knew of its location was me and my attorney. No one had ever visited. Not even my mother. It was the only place I had where I could truly relax and switch off. It was my own personal sanctuary. Without it, I would have lost my mind.

I walked out of the room and headed toward my bedroom, barely even glancing at the African masks that adorned the hallway leading to my exclusive wing of the house. They always freaked me out if I looked at them too closely. I felt as if there were African spirits contained in their empty faces, waiting to come out and ask me why I had such a large collection of Yoruba and Maasai masks when I'd never so much as visited the African continent.

As I reached my bedroom, I pulled out my phone and saw two missed calls. One was from my mother and the other one, well, the other one was from someone I had no wish to speak to ever again.

I threw the phone onto my mattress and walked into the bathroom, pulling my clothes off as I walked. I turned on the shower and stood underneath the too-hot water, letting it scald my skin as if that would somehow help to cleanse me of all the things I hated about myself.

CHAPTER 2

P<small>IPER</small>

"On my way."
"Hurry," I typed back, slightly annoyed.
"Tonight we're going to get laid."
"Are you sure you didn't already?"
"Nope, date was a bore."
"Oh?"
"I'll tell you all over a cocktail."
"Hurry, I'm falling asleep."
"Nearly there."
"Where are you??"

The last text had been sent over an hour ago, and I was debating whether or not to just leave the club. The night was starting out with as much promise as an almost empty fridge with a lone, moldy apple sitting in it. It was ten-thirty and my best friend, Alexa, still hadn't arrived.

I stifled a yawn as I looked around the hot new club,

surrounded by pulsing young bodies that were high on life, alcohol, and drugs. The bass of the music felt too loud to my ears, but I knew that was because I was an old fart at the grand age of twenty-eight. My black dress felt too tight and too skimpy, and my heels were already hurting my feet. I was ready to go home, but I knew Alexa would kill me if I went back to the hotel room before the night had even started.

I looked at my phone again to see if she'd responded to my last text message. When she'd told me she would meet me at the club because she was going to meet a guy from Tinder for a drink in Beverly Hills, I'd thought it was a good idea, but now I wasn't so sure. Maybe she should have just met me back at the hotel room. I walked toward the bar, debating between getting myself shit-faced drunk and just enjoying the night or going home and watching *Friends*. I closed my eyes for a few seconds and let the music pulse past me. I could almost imagine that I fit in with all the hot young things dancing around, but I knew that was just an illusion.

My eyes popped open as I felt someone brushing past me and it took a while for me to adjust back to the strobe lights and laughing mannequins that surrounded me.

I reached my hand up to touch my hair to see if it still felt silky and smooth or if it had frizzed up in the sweaty heat of the club. I was pleased to feel soft tresses beneath my fingers and smiled to myself. At least one thing was going right tonight.

I wandered around the sides of the club, nodding my head to the beat of the music. The vibe in the club was contagious, and I wanted to go dancing in the crowds, but I didn't really want to go by myself. It would be much more fun with Alexa. As I walked past two girls drinking lemon drop cocktails, I thought back to the strange man I'd met earlier in the cupcake store. The interaction had been so weird, but he'd stuck with me. I'd barely been able to tell what he'd looked like, but his personality had been witty, and surprisingly I'd found myself quite attracted to him.

Especially when he'd whispered in my ear. In fact, I'd been quite shocked at how turned on I'd been at the feel of his warm breath. I'd been disappointed when he just ran out of the store. Even though I hadn't seen his face and he'd had the weirdest redneck mustache, he had sported a body that was fitter than fit and, well, I'd had a feeling that he'd quite fancied me as well. I sighed as I felt my body growing warm at my thoughts. I needed to find somebody real to hook up with. That guy was long gone.

I was doing a look over in the crowd to see if Alexa had made it yet when two tall blonde girls brushed past me giggling as they danced to the Pitbull song pumping through the speakers.

"And so I said to Zoila, well, duh, I'm going to take the audition, I mean, it's for Scorsese," blonde number one said.

"No way, Martin Scorsese?" Blonde number two gawked at her.

"No." Tall blonde number one laughed. "Big Boobs Scorsese, you know, the guy that does those Spring Break videos."

"Oh yeah, yeah, he's rich." Blonde number two grinned at her. "I think I saw he was a judge at Martini's wet T-shirt contest last week. My friend Lisa won. She got like, five hundred dollars and a free T-shirt."

I pressed my lips together to stop myself from laughing and turned away from them, about to pull out my phone to text Alexa that I was going to leave. This club was far out of my comfort zone, and I just wasn't having fun at all. I wasn't even in a dancing mood, if I was honest with myself. And not one of the young hot studs milling around had so much as glanced at me.

"Would you like a drink?"

The words were smooth and sexy. I turned to brush off

my suitor with a small smile. I never accepted drinks from strangers. It just wasn't smart. How were you to know that they hadn't dropped a roofie in it or something? I didn't want to end up in the back of a car I didn't know. But even though I was going to say no to the drink, I was happy to have been asked.

"N ... Oh." My eyes made contact with the man who had offered me the drink and my jaw dropped.

"Is oh a yes or a no?"

His eyes twinkled as he smiled down at me, obviously having had this reaction from multiple women throughout his life. I blinked rapidly as I stared back up at him. I could barely believe my eyes. Jackson Camden was standing in front of me. *The* Jackson Camden. The rock star Jackson Camden. Jackson Camden of my teenage dreams and, if I'm honest, several late-night fantasies.

"I, uh..." I mumbled and swallowed hard as I shook my head. "I..." I started again, but my voice trailed off as I noticed that I had lost his attention already.

"Jackson Camden, is that you?" A tall, slinky blonde joined us at the bar and ran her fingers down his back as she purred up at him, lips pouted and boobs pressing into him. I had to admit that I was slightly envious of her confidence. There was no way that I would feel comfortable pushing myself on a famous rock star like that.

"Yes, it's me." He had completely turned away from me now, and I watched as he smiled at her.

"Can I have your autograph?"

I watched as she giggled and flirted with him. I couldn't look away even though I was starting to feel like a bit of a voyeur.

"Sure, where do you want it?" He took the pen from her hand and my jaw dropped once again as the lady pulled her top down and asked him to sign her breast.

"Better luck next time," a voice whispered into my ear from behind me. I jumped, let out a small scream, and dropped my purse in surprise. I bent down to pick it up.

"Excuse me?" I glared up at the man next to me, not looking at him properly as I stood back up, clutching my bag tightly to my chest. Had he been watching me watch Jackson and the blonde this whole time?

"I said, better luck next time." His voice was deep and mocking, and his tone was already irritating me.

"Better luck next time?" I finally made contact with his sharp, azure blue eyes and my heart skipped a beat as I realized who I was talking to. The number one actor in all of Hollywood, Oracle Lion. He looked taken aback as our eyes made contact, and he seemed to be searching for something in my gaze. I offered him a small smile, but he didn't smile back and I stood there, feeling uncomfortable.

"Just think, that could have been your breast he was signing if you'd been able to open your mouth a bit faster." His lips twisted up at the side and he looked as cocky in person as I had always imagined him to be from his movie posters and TV interviews.

"I don't want him signing my breasts." I spoke stiffly, not knowing what to say. I wanted to tell him off for being rude, but how did you tell off a big star?

"You'd rather have him doing other things to your breasts?" He grinned and licked his lips in a deeply suggestive manner. I shuddered in response. My shudder was directed to both him and myself. I couldn't believe that he would be so blatant with me, and I couldn't believe that I sort of liked it. Most probably because of my earlier flirtation, my body was in high gear.

"No!" I said sharply. "That's really out of order."

"What is?" he said with a small wink. "You need to loosen up, lady." He stared at my lips and I wanted to slap the smirk off of his face. "Or maybe you need something sweet to eat." He said the words slowly and suggestively.

There was something in the way that he spoke that sounded so familiar to me, but I shook it off as just being smitten with his movies. Instead of responding to him, I turned away from him. I was pleased to see that the blonde was gone. Jackson was still there, and I took a deep breath before tapping on his shoulder.

"I'll have that drink now." I smiled up at him and he looked back at me with a smile.

"I thought you'd never say yes," he teased with a crooked smile, and I laughed loudly so that the other man would see that I could be fun, even if he didn't think so.

"Aren't you going to introduce me to your friend, Jackson?" The man behind me said, and I groaned.

Why was he still here? Though I could probably guess. He was obviously there with Jackson. I didn't know that they were friends, but didn't all famous people seem to know each other? Thinking about it, hadn't they been in a band together years ago?

"Sure, if I can get her name."

Jackson grinned at me, and I felt my face flush with pleasure. It was kind of cool that a hot rock star wanted to know my name. Actually, it was more than kind of cool, it was super cool and awesome, and I wanted to text Alexa and jump up and down. Nothing like this had ever happened to me before in my life.

"Piper." I smiled at him sweetly, my heart racing rapidly. "I'm Piper."

"Peter Piper picked a peck of pickled peppers," began the man behind me, and I ignored him. He was trying to rile me up for some reason. I just didn't know why.

"Nice name." Jackson smiled at me. "I'm Jackson, and that's my good friend, Oracle."

I turned around reluctantly and looked at the annoying man behind me again. This time I allowed my eyes to look him over fully, while he did the same to me.

Of course, I had known as soon as I'd seen him that he was Oracle Lion. I would have had to have lived under a rock not to know who he was. Oracle Lion was an A-list actor, former rock star, and a complete and utter playboy. He was in the newspaper almost every other week with a different model or actress on his arms. And he was known as the most eligible bachelor in Hollywood. He was sex on legs, and standing next to him I felt his presence and charisma oozing from every pore of his body.

If it had been hard to believe that Jackson Camden was here, then it was even harder to believe that the handsome, gorgeous, and completely untameable Oracle Lion was standing right next to me. It was hard to believe, but it was true. I guess the gossip rags weren't always true. They said that Oracle never deigned to go to public establishments anymore. He only liked to attend exclusive parties and private clubs.

I guess they'd been wrong.

"Hi, what's your name again?" Oracle held his hand out and tilted his head as he gave me a small nod.

"Like I just said, I'm Piper." I reached my hand out to shake his, and I felt a small buzz as our fingers touched. "And you are?" I gave him a small smile, faking politeness as he grinned. "I didn't quite catch your name. Did Jackson say Urkel?" I gave him a blank stare, hoping he bought my I-have-no-idea-who-you-are-act.

"No, I'm not Urkel." He raised an eyebrow as he stared at me with the most intense gaze I'd ever experienced in my life. His blue eyes seemed to sparkle as he kept his focus on me. "I'm the starring fantasy of every woman's dreams."

He winked at me, and I was glad that I had faked ignorance. He was an insufferable bore with an ego bigger than the sun. I could tell that already. And just because he was hot didn't mean I was going to fall at his feet. I was over assholes, famous or not.

"Oh, is that your name? It's pretty long, isn't it?" I raised an eyebrow at him and his eyes narrowed as he stared at me. The cocky smile left his face and I could see that he was taken aback.

"Yes, it is pretty long, but I usually save that talk for the bedroom." Oracle's expression turned seductive, and I swallowed hard as I thought about being in his bedroom with both of us naked.

"Whatever, Urrrkkkeeel," I said, pretending that he hadn't gotten me hot and bothered. "Were you named after Steve Urkel from *Family Matters*?"

"You're joking, right?" Oracle smirked at me, and I responded with a blank face.

I couldn't stand cocky guys. Especially guys like Oracle who thought they were God's gift to women. I knew all about Oracle Lion. Everyone who owned a TV or saw a magazine knew that he had more women than some people had acquaintances. I wasn't going to let him think I was going to be his next conquest.

"Joking about what?" I shrugged and looked over at Jackson who was observing the conversation with a huge grin.

"I think you've finally met someone who doesn't know who you are, pal." Jackson started laughing and punched Oracle in the shoulder.

"Yes, it would seem that way." Oracle looked into my eyes and this time he smiled sweetly. I could see why so many women fell for him; his very glance made me feel like he was gazing directly into my soul. "You don't recognize me at all, do you?" His tone was curious as he tilted his head to look at me in a way that made me shiver. Was he really so full of himself that he thought I wouldn't recognize him?

"So what would you like to drink, Piper?" Jackson asked me again, and I was about to answer when I felt my phone vibrating through my purse. I pulled it out and saw that it was Alexa. Finally!

"Where you at, biatch? I'm here." That was Alexa—always so polite.

"Excuse me, sorry. I think my friend is here," I said as I texted her back.

"Hey, I'm inside by the bar."

"Cool, get me a drink."

"What do you want?"

"White wine. Or a White Russian. Or both. Or white wine with a white Russian in a hot tub. :)"

"Okay. Also, you will never guess who is here!" I typed and prayed that Oracle wasn't spying on me and staring at my screen while I typed.

"Who??? Putin?"

"Alexa! I'm rolling my eyes. Putin?"

"Ha ha, then who?"

You'll see. See ya in a few," I typed and put my phone back in my purse.

"So was that your boyfriend?" Jackson asked, his eyes on my hands as I shook my head, my face covered in a goofy smile. Alexa always made me laugh, even when I was mad at her for being late.

"No, it's my best friend, Alexa." I could feel Oracle staring at me, but I didn't look at him. "We've treated ourselves to a ladies' weekend," I explained, even though he hadn't asked me any other questions. "I'm surprised to see you here. I thought you were based in New York."

To be honest, I had no idea if Jackson was based in NYC or LA, and I didn't really care. However, I knew for a fact that Oracle was based in LA because I'd read an article only a couple weeks prior about some new ten-million-dollar house he'd bought in Studio City. The exterior had been beautiful, but the inside looked like a hot mess, full of ostentatious pop art and artifacts that belonged in a museum, not a home.

Not that I would tell him that, no way, José I wasn't going to admit that I was an avid reader of gossip mags and had more than once had a crush on a movie star when I was younger, including him. He couldn't know that I knew what his bedroom looked like, not when I'd pretended that I didn't even know who he was.

"Ladies' weekend?" he asked me, and I have to admit that I was surprised that he was showing any sort of interest in my life.

"Piper, Piper, there you are!"

Alexa ran over to me, bumping past people without a care as she made her way to me, her long blond hair flowing down her back. She was wearing a very short red dress and four-inch heels. Her mascara was caked on blacker than I'd ever seen it and her red lipstick screamed, *Look at my pouty lips!* She looked like she was hoping to be discovered and featured on the cover of *Playboy* magazine and I couldn't help smiling. We were such opposites.

"I have been looking all over for you." She gave me a huge hug, and I knew she hadn't noticed Jackson or Oracle as yet, even though they were standing right next to me and staring at us both.

"I highly doubt you've been looking that long as you just arrived a minute ago." I laughed as we air-kissed.

"So where's my wine and Putin?"

"Alexa." I rolled my eyes at her. "No one would ever believe you were a grad student at Berkeley."

"Stop being so kind, Piper." She winked at me and then she gasped and I knew that she had spotted at least one, if not both of the famous men next to me. "Oracle Lion, is that you? Oh my God!" She almost screamed as she stared at Oracle, and I knew he was grinning even without looking at his face. "Is this who you were talking about, Piper?" She grinned at me. "I knew this was the place to be."

"How do you do?" Oracle's voice was smooth as he spoke to Alexa. "I assume you're Pepper's best friend?"

"Pepper?" Alexa looked confused. "You mean Piper?"

"Oh, yes, that was it." I looked over at him now and I could see the smug look on his face as his eyes danced along my face. "Piper, of course." He gave me a fake apologetic smile, and I did my best not to roll my eyes at him.

"And I'm Jackson." Jackson moved from next to me and inserted himself right next to Alexa. "Nice to make your acquaintance."

"You too. I'm Alexa." Alexa grinned and then looked at me with a searching look as if to ask, *How did this happen?*

I shrugged at her. I wasn't sure why Jackson had approached me, and I was still quite shocked that more women hadn't come up to the two of them. I mean, here they were, two huge megastars—but then I remembered that we were in West Hollywood and the last thing anyone did was approach stars. It just wasn't done, though I could feel the stares of half the club on us now. I had been oblivious to the stares before because I'd been so annoyed waiting for Alexa, but now I could clearly see that both men and women were staring at the four of us with varying degrees of jealousy, surprise, excitement, and wonder. I could see the women wondering what Alexa and I had that they didn't. They wanted to know how we were so lucky as to grab two of the hottest men in Hollywood's attention. I wasn't sure myself, but I wasn't going to question it.

"Would you like a drink?"

"Oh..." She looked at me before answering. I could tell

from the look on her face that she wanted to say yes. I knew that she fancied Jackson. I mean, who wouldn't? But he was a rock star with a well-known penchant for one-night stands, and I didn't see what the point of them getting to know each other would be. We'd be driving back up to Northern California the next day. "What do you think, Piper?"

"I think Piper wants you to say no. She wants you all to herself." Oracle winked at me and then continued. "And I can see why, you're one sexy woman, Alexa."

"Excuse me?" I blinked at him, my eyes narrowing. "What does that mean?"

"What does what mean?" He stared at me then, a small curve on the right side of his lips. "Are you saying that you would like to have a drink with us?"

"Well, no, that's not what I'm saying, but ..."

"So you'd rather have Alexa all to yourself?"

"Why are you putting it like that?" I glared at him. "Like I'm ..." My lips stopped moving as I could see that he was looking close to laughter.

"Like you're what?" he questioned.

"Like I'm a lesbian."

"Is there anything wrong with being a lesbian?"

"No, of course not, that's not what I'm saying."

"I quite think that I'd be a lesbian if I were to become a woman," he said with a huge grin. "I'd be a huge dyke."

"You can't say that." I shook my head at him. "You just love being controversial, don't you?"

"Am I controversial?" he asked, one eyebrow raised as he moved closer to me. "I don't find myself to be very controversial."

"I think I'll accept that drink," Alexa said to Jackson, giving me a small smile. "Seems like you two are busy chatting."

"We're *not* busy chatting."

I gave her a look, but she smiled sweetly for a second and then whispered something in Jackson's ear. He looked back at me and Oracle and started laughing. I could feel myself growing heated as I knew they were laughing at me. What had she said to him? And what happened to girl code? Alexa should have been guiding me to the other side of the club or even out of it as soon as she saw how rude Oracle was being to me.

"Where are you going?" I asked as she stepped back.

"Piper, please," she mouthed at me, her light brown eyes twinkling as she gave me a look that said, *Please, please do not ruin this for me.*

And I knew I had to suck it up. How often did either one of us have a hot, handsome A-lister interested in us, even if it was just for a hookup? Never, that was how often. Not that we were ugly or anything, but we were both just that bit too nerdy to attract loads of men.

Well, I was too nerdy, at least. Alexa always got men. Even though she had been a history major like me, she didn't look like the typical history buff. Not many people would guess that she was getting her PhD in European history. She didn't even give off that sexy librarian vibe when her hair was in a bun. She was cute and fun-loving and sexy, but she was also very astute and aware of the opposite sex. She knew how to flirt and she knew how to flirt well. Unlike me. I was the definition of awkwardness, and I couldn't flirt to save my life.

"Fine, I'll have a Moscow mule, please."

I gave her a pointed look that said, *You better not just disappear on me.* She was definitely going to hear it from me as it had been her idea for us to come down to LA for the weekend to have a break. We'd rented an Airbnb and gone shopping in San Francisco at the Westfield Mall for some new outfits to wear. I'd even gone to the hairdresser to get a blowout, even though my naturally curly hair had a mind of its own. We'd planned to go driving around the Hollywood Hills and then to Beverly Hills to look at stars' homes. Then we were going to go to Santa Monica and Venice Beach to check out the piers. We weren't going to swim, though, because you didn't get a seventy-five-dollar blowout just to wash it out in with dunk in the water.

We'd planned to write at some coffee shops and check out bookstores and then have a fun night out dancing and flirting with wannabe actors. I should have known that everything had sounded too good to be true. We'd left Oakland in my car and driven down the I-5 singing Ed Sheeran and Rihanna songs, ignoring the bad drivers who sped past us to only have to slow down when they hit the inevitable traffic that flooded the interstate between the Bay Area and Los Angeles.

Everything had been great until we'd arrived at the Airbnb and realized that we only had one actual bedroom and the other bed was a couch with a foldout mattress in the living room. We'd flipped a coin for the bedroom and I'd won.

I had taken a shower and when I'd come out of the bathroom, Alexa was standing there with a guilty but excited look on her face. She'd told me that she'd downloaded Tinder and had matched with several guys and that one had already asked her to meet up. When she'd asked if I minded her meeting him for a quick bite and drink before we went to the club, I hadn't been happy, but what could I say? The fact that she'd taken hours on the date and now was flitting off with some new man minutes after she'd arrived at the club had me fuming. I didn't see the point of even being here if all she'd wanted was to hook up with some guy. What sort of girl's trip started and ended with a hookup?

"Okay," she said and she disappeared to another side of the bar with Jackson Camden leading the way, his hand on her back. I pursed my lips and stifled a sigh as I saw her looking up at him with a winning flirtatious smile.

"So, what happens between the two people left behind when their best friends leave them to go and hook up?" Oracle whispered into my ear as I continued to watch Alexa and Jackson walk away into the flashing lights.

"They haven't left us to hook up." I looked up at him, annoyed at the smug look on his face.

"Are you jealous?" There was a smirk on his face.

"Jealous about what?"

"That Jackson ditched you as soon as your friend arrived?"

"He didn't ditch me," I said, but then I thought about the situation. He had been flirting with me initially, but as soon as he'd seen Alexa, he'd moved on. That should have made me jealous, but frankly, I was too annoyed to care. Yes, Jackson Camden was hot, but he wasn't really my type. He seemed too out there for me.

"Aww, okay. Yeah, that's you walking to the VIP section with him to have some champagne on the house." Oracle nodded. "Sorry, I forgot."

"You really are an asshole, aren't you?"

"Am I?" He cocked his head to the side and smiled, the light never catching his eyes. "I don't know about that. How's about we make the most out of tonight and have a little fun?"

"Are you joking?" I almost laughed at the look on his face. "Do you really think that I'm going anywhere with you?"

"We can cut the crap," he said as he moved closer to me, his lips almost next to mine as he stared into my eyes. "I know you know who I am. You'd have to live under a rock to not know. Let's stop playing games and just cut to the chase."

"Does that normally work for you?" I licked my lips nervously as I spoke back to him. I couldn't lie to myself. He was sexy and his blue eyes seemed to be looking directly into my soul. I'd never been so close to a man this handsome before and it made me nervous. If I was a different kind of girl, I'd definitely say yes to going back to his place for one night. I mean, how many people got to say they hooked up with a huge star?

But then again, this was Oracle Lion, so probably a lot of women.

"Do most women accept my offer of a hookup?" He chuckled as if the question I'd asked him was a joke. "Let's just say most women don't even wait for me to offer, it usually comes from them ... Do you know how many panties I've been given?"

"And you like that?" I said disdainfully. He really was a pig. "You just take them home with you."

"I don't take anyone to my home," he said, his lips thin. "I'm not inviting you to my home."

"So, where do you propose we have this hot sex then?"

"Well, I didn't say it would be sex, and I certainly didn't say it would be hot, but I like the way your mind thinks." He bit down on his lower lip and his mouth moved closer to my ear. "If you want to invite me back to your place to show you how hot it could be, let me know."

"I don't think so."

"Well, then what do two people who have been ditched by their friends do?" he asked and his hand moved to my hair and started stroking it back behind my ear.

His warm fingers on my skin felt nice, but as I looked at his face, I could see a distant look in his expression. I could have been anyone at that moment. I meant absolutely nothing to him. I could tell that I was just another woman to him. I was upset at that, but what was I expecting? That after ten minutes of chatting, I'd be special to him?

"They go home and relax in a big comfy bed," I said matter-of-factly.

A part of me was annoyed with Alexa—we hadn't had a girl's night out in ages—but the other part of me was quite happy and excited for her. If she was going to ditch me, I'm glad it was to be with a hottie like Jackson. He looked like the sort of guy that could show her a good time, and she was in need of one of them.

Both of us had been in a rut recently; our love lives were almost nonexistent, jobs and school weren't satisfying, and at twenty-eight years of age, we were both at a bit of a standstill. That's why we'd decided on this super fun weekend away, and I supposed this would help her, even if it didn't help me, but oh well, I'd have plenty of fun in the Airbnb. I would enjoy watching Netflix and eating greasy pizza that I'd order from some online food delivery place.

"Oh, is that an invite or a hint for an invite?" I felt Oracle's hand on the small of my back.

I gave him a look of distaste and stepped away. "Neither." I stared at him for a few seconds and then grinned at the complete and utter confusion that had crossed his face. "I meant, we go back to our individual places and sleep in our individual beds."

"Alone?" His brows furrowed.

"Yes, alone," I said slowly and then just in case he didn't understand. "I'm not hooking up with you, Oracle Lion."

"But let's be real here, did I ask you to, Prickly Piper?"

He gave me a disarming smile, and I just stared at his handsome face for a few seconds. I could understand why he was so popular. But I also knew I wasn't his type. He went for sleek, skinny blondes who hung on his every word. I was five eight, with curves, a stomach that had never seen a six-pack, long black curly hair, and a mouth that lived to challenge everything he'd ever thought about women.

"No, you didn't, but I assumed that was the purpose of you trying to garner an invitation back to my hotel room."

"Hotel room?" He blinked. "You don't live in LA?"

"No." I laughed. "I'm based in Northern California."

"Oh?" He smiled briefly as he nodded to himself. I

wondered what he was thinking about and what he'd been agreeing with himself about. "Are you going to say where?"

"No." I shrugged. "Does it matter?"

"You don't like me, do you?" He seemed genuinely interested in my answer.

"I don't know you. I don't feel any way about you."

"You don't fancy me?"

"Fancy you? What are you, English?"

"Actually, yes." He grinned. "My mom is English. Well, kind of."

"Oh."

I hadn't known that, but I couldn't express surprise because then I'd be admitting that I knew who he was in the first place. And what did he mean by kind of? How could you "kind of" be English?

"But don't change the subject. Don't you fancy me?" He stepped closer to me and I felt a warm feeling curling in my belly as I waited for him to touch me. The anticipation was killing me, and I knew that I was all over the place in my mind and in my heart; I told myself that I didn't want him to touch me, but my whole body was anticipating it.

"You're handsome, if that's what you're asking, but you know that. I'm just not interested in whatever you have to offer." I grabbed the glass that was in his hand and downed all of it. It was so uncharacteristic of me and I think I shocked both him and myself. "And with that, I think I'm going to head home."

"Do you want a ride?"

Oracle looked gobsmacked at my words and I wanted to laugh. I couldn't seriously be the first woman to turn down his advances, could I?

"Nope, no, nein." I shook my head and looked around the club to see if I could see Alexa.

She was nowhere in sight, and I wasn't just going to stand

around waiting for her. She could do what she wanted with Jackson. I wasn't going to be some fool who just waited around on her. She was a big girl and could take care of herself. She'd already wasted enough of my time this evening, and I wasn't going to allow her to waste any more of it. I'd speak to her in the morning about how much she'd disappointed me, but for now, I was out.

"Well, I would say it was nice meeting you, but ..." Oracle stared at me for a few seconds, and I laughed loudly.

"Same. I would say it but it wouldn't be true, would it?" I lifted my hand and gave him a small wave. "See ya!"

I turned around and exited the club as quickly and gracefully as I could, with my head held up. I could feel his eyes on me as I left and I so badly wanted to look back to see if he was staring at me, but I didn't want to give him that satisfaction.

As I made my way through the crowds of people waiting to get into the club, disappointment hit me. Maybe I had made a mistake. Maybe I should have accepted his offer. My life was in a rut and I needed a change and it wasn't like I didn't think he was hot as hell.

I sighed as I walked toward Santa Monica Boulevard so that I could catch an Uber in a less packed area. It didn't matter now. I had already left the club, and it wasn't like he'd come running after me. I laughed at that thought. Imagine if he had come running out after me; while that would have seemed romantic in a movie, it would have been creepy in real life. So creepy. And at least I'd left having rejected him. I'd taken him down a peg or two, and that made me feel good. He was way too cocky for his own good. Way too cocky.

Just because he was a hot movie star didn't mean he could just get anyone he wanted.

CHAPTER 3

ORACLE

Of course, I'd known Piper was the woman from the cupcake shop as soon as I'd seen her chatting with Jackson. She'd stepped up her game tonight, wearing a slinky tight dress that left nothing to the imagination. As soon as I'd seen her there, smiling and laughing, I'd grown hard and perhaps a little jealous of Jackson. I'd been happy when she'd dismissed him, though I'd been surprised that she'd given me such a frosty reception. She'd been so open and sweet in the cupcake store. But then that had been when she'd thought I was someone else. Now she'd met me as Oracle, she hadn't seemed as carefree and warm. In retrospect, she'd had quite a bit of an attitude towards me.

Now the woman with the blazing brown eyes was sprinting out of the club as she fled from me. I was amused at her obvious lie about not knowing who I was. I'd seen the way her eyes had widened as she'd seen me for the first time. She'd known who I was. I knew that for a fact. What surprised me was that she had pretended not to know me and then had dismissed my offer of getting to know her better. Women never dismissed me. Normally, they were all over me.

Piper was a bit of an anomaly. She had been dressed up for a night on the town and had looked stunning with her long black wavy locks and deep brown eyes. Many of the men in the club had noticed her just as Jackson and I had, but she'd seemed oblivious to all of us.

There had been genuine shock and pleasure on her face when Jackson had spoken to her. And what looked like awe. An awe she hadn't expressed when she'd noticed me. I had to admit that I was a bit pissed off that she'd blatantly dismissed me, even when her friend had almost jumped into Jackson's arms. It seemed to me that Piper was a woman who very much needed a good fucking to loosen her up. I'd have been willing to take on the job, but obviously, she didn't know a good time when it presented itself. Not that I cared. She was insignificant in my world and life. I'd never see her again, and I'd most probably never think of her again, either. I looked around the club to see if I could spy Jackson anywhere or if I should leave, but before I had time to make my move to peruse the club, two redheads approached me.

"Oracle Lion, is that you?" The tall one with the big green eyes touched my shoulder. "I can't believe it's really you!"

"Who else would I be?" I said blinking at her, no smile on my face.

"You're funny." The other one had an eager smile on her slightly chubby face as she looked up at me. "Oracle Lion, who knew you were so funny?"

"Obviously, not I," I said and withheld a sigh as they both burst out laughing. "But apparently to you two, I'm the next Chris Rock or Richard Pryor."

"Richard who?" The tall redhead said, confused.

"You know who, Cindy. The guy who owns that airline and that private island."

"Richard Branson?" I looked around the room, annoyed. On most nights, I didn't care how dumb and ditzy the women were that I slept with, but I wasn't in the mood right now. I needed to find Jackson and see if he was still with Piper's friend. Maybe she could give me some more information on why Piper had been so rude.

"So ... I'm an actress as well." The chubby girl batted her eyelids at me. "I'd love to audition for you sometime. Like at your place or something ..." She grinned up at me hopefully. "I'm even free tonight."

"I don't think so." I shook my head and almost sighed in relief as Jackson and Alexa came back into sight. "Hey." I beckoned to Jackson, and I could see the huge grin on his face as he took in the sight before him.

"Oracle Lion, my word. I leave you behind for ten minutes and you've already got yourself a harem of ladies." Jackson slapped me on the shoulder and I watched as the two redheads jaws dropped in major excitement. I looked over at Alexa, who had a bemused expression on her face as she stood there sipping a fruity looking cocktail.

"Where's Piper?" she asked casually, no actual worry or concern on her face.

"She left," I said with a small shrug. "She seemed to think that you and Jackson had disappeared for the night ... not that I can blame her." I looked over at Jackson and then back at Alexa in her tight little dress.

"I didn't leave her." Alexa cursed under her breath and handed me her drink. "Hold this, please, I need to text her."

"Sure, sure," I said holding the drink and turning my back to the two redheads that Jackson was now flirting with outrageously. I wondered if Alexa felt jealous or sad that she had already lost his attention. Jackson Camden was notorious for his one-night stands, and he often had multiple ones in a single night. I thought I was bad about relationships, but

Jackson didn't seem to care about women at all. The way he treated them and their feelings was pretty horrific, even by my standards, but that didn't seem to stop women from wanting him.

"Shit, she's gone." Alexa shook her head and sighed, her eyes meeting mine with an exasperated look. "Why didn't you talk to her or something?"

"I did talk to her." I stared back at her, my face expressionless. "She wanted to leave."

"Fuck it." She nibbled on her lower lip and glanced over at Jackson. I could tell from her face that she was having a moral dilemma. Should she leave now and go and make things right with her best friend? Or should she stay and have a shot at a night with Jackson? I had a pretty good guess at which direction she was going to take. They all took the same path when it came to Jackson.

"She's a big girl. I'm sure she'll be okay," I said as I handed her back her drink.

"We came to LA together though." She actually looked guilty and I was surprised to see that she was still anxiously texting Piper. Maybe she was a better friend than I'd initially thought. "I think I'm going to have to go."

"You're going to go?" I said, my voice loud to alert Jackson. He was still chatting with the redheads, but I was pretty sure that Alexa would make for a better night than them. If I hadn't seen Piper first, I might have been attracted to her myself. She was beautiful in an obvious kind of way, while Piper had an understated sexiness to her. Piper had layers that I wanted to peel back in more ways than one.

She nodded as she sipped on her drink. "Yeah, I think so. She's my best friend and, well, I already ditched her once tonight. I should go and catch up with her."

"You're leaving?" Jackson looked pained and I could tell that he realized he'd messed up. His back was now to the two redheads who were standing there looking like they didn't know what was going on. "Stay." He put his hand on Alexa's shoulder and started massaging her back. "I promise we'll have fun."

"I have to go and find Piper."

"Oh." He looked taken aback and slightly annoyed. "Oracle, can't you find her?"

"She left."

"Oh, well then, she left." He shrugged and looked at Alexa. "Catch up with her tomorrow."

"No, I have to make sure she got home okay." Alexa shook her head. "She's my best friend. We're not from LA."

"She'll be fine. She's a big girl." Jackson used the same words that had come out of my mouth, and I wondered if they'd sounded as condescending when I'd said them. I frowned as he continued trying to persuade her to stay. Is this what we'd come to?

"Jackson, dude. If she wants to go, let her go."

"Let us at least give you a ride?" Jackson asked.

It surprised me that he'd be willing to leave the club to help her until I realized that his offer was really one that would benefit him. Because after we gave her a ride, I was sure he'd be offering to then take her back to his place, or in this case, my place, seeing as he was staying with me.

"Oh, are you sure?" Alexa positively jumped at the idea and I could see Jackson flashing her a smile as he winked at me. He had another one in the bag.

"Am I sure? I've never been surer." He sounded so confident when he spoke that I couldn't stop myself from smiling. "Hey, Oracle, you mind driving us?"

"No, it's fine," I said with a grunt. I was ready to leave the club and get home. I had some scripts that I wanted to read and I had a call with my mother in the morning that I knew would drain me. "Let's go."

I didn't want to admit to myself that I was also curious about Piper and that I wanted to see her again. I also wondered if it was smart to let Alexa go with Jackson. He was my best friend and he was a good guy, but he wasn't the sort of guy that could give any woman what she really wanted. All he did was break hearts, but I figured Alexa couldn't be expecting a ring or anything. She wasn't that naive, surely?

"Thank you so much." Alexa clutched my arm and gave me a grateful look. I was surprised by the sincere smile on her face. "This means a lot to me. I'm having fun with you guys, but you know ..." Her voice trailed off and she looked embarrassed. I knew what she was thinking. She wanted to be a good friend, but she also wanted to hook up with Jackson. I couldn't fault her for that. The allure of being with an A-list star wasn't lost on many people.

"No worries. Has she responded to your text messages?"

"No, she hasn't." She shook her head. "I have a feeling she's mad at me."

"Maybe she's just mad at the world."

"What do you mean?" Alexa blinked at me, her face a mix of surprise and agreement.

"Nothing. She just seems like a hard woman to get to know."

"Did she shoot you down?" Jackson laughed then. "Is that what this is all about?"

"She didn't shoot me down," I denied, somewhat angry and defensive.

"Don't worry. It's not personal to you." Alexa gave me a small smile. "Piper doesn't really date, and when she does, it's with intellectual guys. She's not one to go for good looks and Hollywood charm."

"I see." While her words should have made me feel better, they made me feel more annoyed. As if I was upset that Piper hadn't wanted to hook up. She wasn't even my normal type.

"Let's go and see if we can find your nerdy friend then," I said and with that, I was strolling ahead of them out of the club. I was over the night. Over the drinks. Over the loud music. Over the women staring and fawning at me. I was over all of it. I just wanted to leave and make sure that a certain raven-haired beauty was tucked safely in bed so that I could let her know that I had absolutely no interest in ever actually sharing it with her.

CHAPTER 4

PIPER

"Hey, are you mad at me?"
"Piper, answer me. I'm worried."
"I only went to get a drink I was coming back."
"Piper!"
"Piper!!!!!!!!"
"Fine, I'm coming back to the Airbnb. Sorry."

I stared at the burst of text messages that Alexa had sent me in the last thirty minutes and smiled. I hadn't responded, not because I was upset with her, but because I hadn't seen them. I'd been stuck in the back of an Uber pool with a very chatty driver and two other passengers. And we'd been engaged in a conversation about the joys of international travel. Each one of us had to come up with our top vacation destination and we'd debated back and forth on the pluses and minuses of Australia (my top destination), Dollywood (a slightly older lady from the South), and Dubai (the uber driver). The conversation had taken my mind off of my night at the club and it wasn't until I'd gotten out of the Uber that I'd seen Alexa's messages.

"Hey, it's okay. I'm just going to order a pizza and then watch some Netflix. Stay out with Jackson Camden and take lots of photos of his naked body. :)"

"Piper, you're alive! Very funny. I'll be back soon."

"Ok."

I wasn't sure if that meant she was on her way back now or if she meant after she hooked up with Jackson, but I didn't care. I was just happy that Alexa had reached out to me. She'd always been a good friend and her texting me meant she was still thinking of our friendship even though she was with a huge rock star. I walked into the lobby of the Airbnb and waited for the elevator.

As I waited, images of Oracle flashed through my mind. He really was a handsome man, even handsomer than he looked on film, and he looked gorgeous on film. I wondered what it would have been like standing here with him, waiting eagerly to go up to my room. Would we have been here kissing? Would his hands have been all over me? Would he have lifted up my skirt as we made our way into the elevator? Would we have had sex in there? My skin felt hot as I pictured my legs wrapped around his waist as he pumped into me, filling me with his hotness.

I shook my head to stop myself from fantasizing about Oracle. Yes, it would have been a once in a lifetime sexual adventure and very much unlike me, but maybe it would have been hot, inspiring and self-awakening. I needed a change in my life to give me some inspiration for my new book, a literary romance with some historical elements. So far, I only had ten thousand words in the book, and they seemed dry and boring.

As the elevator doors opened, I made my way inside with a small smile. Just as the doors were about to close, a handsome man with a dog that he'd obviously just been walking came in.

Oracle and I definitely wouldn't have been having sex in the elevator, then.

"Good evening," the guy said with a brief nod.

I could see he was holding his dog's leash tightly. The big gray dog, I think it was a Weimaraner, looked up at me with large blue eyes and wagged its tail. I smiled at them both and took my place on the other side of the elevator.

"Good evening," I said with a smile back and pressed the floor number. I could hear the dog breathing heavily and I glanced over at him, his gaze still on me.

"Don't mind Fiona, she loves to meet new people." The man grinned as he held her close. "Unfortunately, she doesn't realize that she's too big to jump up on everyone she meets."

"Aww, she's beautiful," I said, glad I hadn't said that Fiona looked like a big boy. "And I wouldn't mind if she jumped up on me. I love dogs."

"Do you have one?"

"No, I wish," I said wistfully. My current lifestyle wasn't conducive to having a dog. Alexa and I rented a pretty small apartment in Lake Merritt, an area in Oakland, and we just didn't have space for a dog. I promised myself when I made more money and could afford a house with a yard that I would get one.

"Maybe one day, then. This is me." He nodded as the elevator stopped and he walked off on the fifth floor. "Sweet dreams."

"You too," I said, and I smiled to myself as the doors closed. It felt nice to have a handsome man smiling and talking with me. It helped to keep my mind off of what could have been with Oracle. The whole evening had been quite fun, even though I hadn't done much. Just the small amount of attention had felt good and that led me to believe that I wasn't spending enough time out of the house. Maybe I was becoming too much of a bore.

I sighed as the elevator stopped and I made my way out of the car, down the corridor, and into the apartment Alexa and I were renting for the weekend. I slipped my heels off as soon as I walked into the apartment and headed toward the living room, switching on the TV for some background noise as I moved through to the bedroom to take my dress off. I unhooked my bra, grabbed a long black Passenger T-shirt and a pair of beach shorts and headed back to the living room to settle on the couch. I relaxed back into the cushions and felt the tension melting away as I looked out the window.

The sky was dark but street lights illuminated the pavement in the distance, and I wondered what was going on in all the apartments in the area. It was amazing to me to think that inside each apartment was a unique person or persons, each one living their different lives. There were so many people in the world with so many dreams, thoughts, and ideas, and yet most of us were limited to only thinking about our own needs and those of our immediate family.

As I sat there, I had an idea for my novel and I wanted to start jotting down some notes but then my stomach started growling. I needed to eat. I was about to call Alexa to see if she wanted me to order her something as well when the door opened.

"Hey, are you hungry?" I called out from the couch as I heard Alexa's footsteps coming into the apartment. "I was thinking of ordering a pizza."

"I wouldn't say no." A deep, familiar voice resonated throughout the room, and I shot up off of the couch.

"You!" I gasped as I stared at Oracle Lion, his face beaming as he took in my appearance: my already messy hair, my short shorts, and the tight T-shirt that had ridden up and was showing off my belly—and the fact that I had no bra on.

"Yes, it's me." He gave me a little wave. I was about to make a snarky comment when Alexa came running into the room followed by Jackson, who stopped next to Oracle.

"Hey, I was worried about you." She gave me a quick hug and took a step back. I could tell from her breath that she'd been drinking quite a bit and her face was flushed and happy. "I told the boys that we needed to come back and make sure you were okay."

"The boys?" I said the words slowly, glancing at her and then at them. The two men stood too tall in the room, they almost seemed to reach the ceiling, and I wondered at their presence here in our cheap little rental. How had Alexa convinced them to come back with her? Surely they had other things to do. They were A-listers, after all.

"Jackson and Oracle." Alexa laughed as she waved back at the two men behind her casually. "You just left the club without a word, we were worried."

"I didn't leave without a word," I said defensively. "You essentially left me to go off with him." I nodded toward Jackson, my face red. "What was I meant to do? Just stand around and wait to see if you were going to hook up with him or not?" My face reddened as I could see both Jackson and Oracle grinning at my words. This was not a conversation I wanted to be having in front of them.

"I told you I was going to get a drink, but oh well," Alexa said with a small laugh. "We're all here now, at least we can hear each other talk."

"I was hoping to take you to a private spot." Jackson stepped forward and placed his hand on her waist. He whispered something into her ear and I had to look away when she started pushing her ass back into him. I knew that Alexa was a little drunk, and she was much more open than I was, but I sure didn't want to see her making out with Jackson or doing anything else.

"Oh, but I don't know that I can leave Piper again." Alexa giggled and looked at me and it was all I could do to stop myself from rolling my eyes.

"I mean, I guess I can just sit here and watch TV and eat pizza alone," I said sarcastically, knowing I was acting like a bit of a spoiled child now.

The smile left Alexa's face and I could tell that she felt bad, which made me feel bad. "I don't want you to be here alone," she said with a small sigh as she took a step away from Jackson.

"I mean, I ..." I was about to tell her to go out and that I'd be fine when Oracle spoke up and interrupted me.

"Don't worry about it. I'll stay here with Piper. Make sure she has some company so you don't feel bad. And I'll even share your pizza, so it doesn't go to waste." Oracle acted like he was doing me some big favor and I was about to protest when he gave me a look. "Unless, of course, Piper says no."

The way he said the words put me in a position where I really couldn't say no. I knew that I could pretend to want to go to bed. I mean it was late, after all. What could he say to that? "No, you can't go to bed"? I hesitated to tell him that I just wanted him to go home. Not just because I wasn't ready to go to bed, but also because I was curious to see what would happen if he stayed.

I must have hesitated too long because he spoke up again before I could reply. "You will let me eat, won't you?"

"Don't think I can say no," I said, my voice stilted as he laughed, a deep low chuckle. I mean, how the hell could I get out of my living room and go to bed after that? Especially because I had a feeling that he had made a double entendre when he'd referred to eating. "But all you'll be eating is pizza," I said with a small smile that made him burst out laughing even harder. "What's so funny?" I gave him my most innocent expression and tried to ignore the racing of my heart as I stared at his body. I could see his muscles through his shirt and while I could lie to him, I couldn't lie to myself. He was hotter than hell, and I would be one very lucky girl if I got to spend a night with him.

"I didn't expect to hear those words coming out of your mouth," he said with a wry smile. "You seem a bit uptight."

"Who, Piper?" Alexa burst out laughing as she observed the banter back and forth between us. "She's the least uptight person you'll ever meet. Did she tell you what she does for a living?"

"No, she didn't." He looked at me curiously. "But I'm hoping she will." He looked me up and down and his eyes seemed to be looking right through me. "All sorts of things are going through my mind now."

"I bet they are." I did a little shimmy and moved my hands up in the air. Let him think I was some sort of stripper or something. I knew his mind was most probably in the gutter.

"Maybe I was wrong about you," he said with a small smile. "And maybe you're wrong about me as well. Maybe neither one of us really knows the other."

"Seeing as we just met a couple of hours ago, I would say that never a truer word was spoken."

"Touché."

His eyes met mine and we just stared at each other for a few seconds. It was a weird feeling looking into the eyes that were so familiar and yet strange to me. I'd watched this man in many movies, fallen in love with his movie persona, and scoffed at his exploits in the tabloids. He was right, of course: I did have preconceived notions about him and didn't know him outside his Hollywood persona. And why had he chosen to stay and eat pizza with me? Surely he had better things to do than chill with a stranger and eat pizza?

"So we're off then." Jackson grabbed Alexa's hand and led her to the door. "See you later, guys."

"Uh, bye."

He led her out of the apartment and I stood there, feeling uneasy. I was letting my best friend leave with a man she barely knew and I was now here with a man I barely knew. What was going on here?

The door slammed as they walked out, and I suddenly became aware that Oracle was laughing, a low, deep chuckle that reverberated through the room. I looked up at him and knew I could take this one of two ways. My brain was screaming at me to tell him to get out and leave me alone, but I had to admit that other parts of me were interested in finding out why he had volunteered to stay.

"So what do you want on your pizza?" I asked him as I headed back to the couch and grabbed my phone. My ears were buzzing and my body felt hot, but I ignored all the warning bells in my head as he walked over and took a seat next to me on the couch.

"How do you feel about anchovies?" he whispered into my ear and I swallowed hard, immediately knowing that I'd made a bad decision. A very bad decision.

CHAPTER 5

Oracle

PIPER'S SKIN felt warm to the touch as my tongue lightly grazed the top of her ear. She seemed to jump a mile as I blew into her ear, and I chuckled slightly as she turned to me.

"What do you think you're doing?" she asked, clearly annoyed. I pulled back immediately and put my hands up.

"Sorry, maybe our wires got crossed."

"Our wires got crossed?" She raised an eyebrow at me and folded her arms. "I don't think our wires got crossed."

"True, neither one of us has wires on us, do we?" I joked. "Maybe our signals got entangled."

"Our signals didn't get entangled." She blinked at me, trying to keep up.

"True, we're not microwaves, maybe our..." I started on my next line but groaned when she sighed audibly.

"Are you always like this?" She shook her head and sank back into the couch. "And what do you want on your pizza? I'm not getting anchovies."

"You're really bossy, aren't you? Do you know who I am, woman?"

"Oh my God, are you serious right now?" She rolled her eyes. "I get it. You're a movie star. Wow, you must be so proud of being the star of the *Babymaker* movies. They're such classic works of art. I like to think of them as the *American Pie* for the current generation." Her voice was light and all I could do was to start laughing at her words. "What's so funny?" Her eyes narrowed as she gazed at me.

"Well, one, you obviously know who I am because I never told you I was in the *Babymaker* movies, and two, I wasn't asking if you knew who I was because I'm a huge movie star, huge in more ways than one, by the way, but because we've met before."

"We've never met before," she scoffed. "Trust me, I'd remember someone with as big a head as yours."

"I didn't say we'd met in the bedroom, but I'm glad you think my head is big. You know what they say, big head, big cock." She gasped and I saw her eyes darting to the front of my pants. "Want a peek to see if it's the head you remember?"

"Oh, my God, you're a pig."

"I'm sorry, I'm sorry. I'm joking." I put my hands up in surrender as she just shook her head at me. "I'm not sure what it is about you that brings out the little boy in me."

"Maybe because you *are* a little boy."

"I can prove to you I'm not." I winked, but then hurriedly continued as she groaned. "But to be fair, you're the one that's making the false claims. I'm not saying you should know me from my films, I'm saying you should know me from earlier today." I changed the timbre in my voice and spoke in a low drawl. "Why, ma'am, you don't remember me, Jethro Clamplett?"

"You mean Jimbo Jethro?" Her jaw dropped. "What? There's no way. How are you Jimbo?"

"It's called being an actor, ma'am."

"You do know that people from North Dakota don't sound like they come from Alabama right?" She started laughing. "I was wondering what was up with the accent and the weird look."

"Weird look? Are you saying that I look weird?"

She considered my face for a moment, and a warm feeling spread through me that I hadn't felt for a while. She seemed to be looking at the real me, and that unnerved me. I hadn't been this unnerved since my first audition, and that had been years ago.

"No, you don't look weird." She shook her head. "So why the disguise, Jimbo Jethro? And why the horrible mustache? I wasn't sure if you were a pedophile or a hillbilly."

"Well, hopefully, you went with hillbilly."

"Yeah." She nodded. "I quite like hillbillies."

"Oh?"

"My grandad grew up in Montana, and he always talked about working on a ranch and riding, and, well ..." She paused for a few seconds. "It always seemed really cool to me. Far away from my life, you know."

"You grew up in California?"

"Yeah, Alexa and I have been friends since elementary school. We grew up in the suburbs of Oakland, near San Francisco. So it was all pretty urban, even though we have the woods nearby."

"Oakland, huh? Isn't that pretty rough?"

"Depends on what part of Oakland you're from, but no, not really. It gets a bad rap in the press, and lately with gentrification and stuff, there are a lot of homeless people, but there are a lot of social issues that surround that, you know." Her voice trailed off. "Sorry, I can get a bit intense at times."

"Hey, no worries, I can see that." She looked embarrassed and I wondered what was on her mind. What was she thinking? She was deeper than the women I normally talked to, and I wasn't quite sure what to say next. Which pissed me off. Had I really forgotten how to talk to an intelligent woman? "So the reason I had a disguise on was because I didn't want to be recognized in the store." I shrugged. "I love being an actor and it has afforded me a lifestyle that I never thought I would ever have, but there are costs that come with being famous, you know."

"Trust me, I can imagine. I think I'd hate to be famous."

"Oh?" I looked at her to see if she was lying. Once again, she had surprised me. Who didn't want to be famous?

"Oh, tell me, Mr. Jimbo Jethro Clampett Oracle Lion, what would you like on your pizza? I'm starving." She bit down on her lower lip and I could see her eyes sparkling. Somehow we'd gotten through the earlier awkwardness of the night.

"I want you,"

I was serious, but I could tell from the expression on her face that she was taken aback. It was too much, too soon.

I wasn't lying at all, though. To hell with pizza, I'd like her flat on her back, legs spread, crying for me to enter her. I didn't care if she wanted my tongue or my cock. I just wanted to taste her and be inside of her. I wanted her to scream my name as if she never wanted to forget it.

"What did you say?" she said, and I could tell that she was getting ready to tell me off.

"I said I want you, but I was joking." I forced a laugh. "You're so easy to wind up, Piper."

"I'm not," she said, and I could see her thinking for a moment. Most probably wondering if she should still tell me off or not. "I think you just like playing games with me, Oracle Lion. I think that you're just mad that I didn't know who you were."

"But we already figured out that you did know who I was."

I pointed my finger at her, and then I said something that shocked me more than it should have. "Also, you can call me Zach."

"Zach?" She looked surprised. "Why Zach?"

"Because that's my name, isn't that obvious?"

"But your name is Oracle ..."

"Do you really think my parents called me Oracle? How many Oracles did you know in school?"

"None," she admitted with a small smile. "So your real name is Zach?"

"Yup."

"I didn't know that."

"Why would you?" I laughed as I realized that once again, unknowingly, she'd revealed that she had actually known who I was all along.

"So you want me to call you Zach instead of Oracle."

"Yeah." I nodded and then grabbed her phone. "And I'm going to choose this pizza now because you're taking forever."

I looked at the screen and the pizza toppings and tried to ignore the voice inside of me that was asking why I'd told her my real name. No one knew my real name. It was the private part of my persona that I saved for those I knew before fame. Not for those I met after. My life pre-Oracle was very different from my life post-Oracle, and it was better that two didn't meet. The only person I had in both worlds was Jackson. Jackson was my man. My best friend. The closest thing I had to a brother. I was lucky that I had him. He knew what it was like to straddle both worlds. He knew what it was like to not be able to trust anyone. Jackson knew me as Zach *and* Oracle, everyone else in my life knew me as one or the other. Everyone else ... except now for Piper.

"Do not pick any anchovies," she growled into my ear and

made me jump slightly this time. I wasn't expected to feel her warm breath in my ear. "You hear me, Zach? No anchovies."

"Okay," I grinned at her. "What about jalapenos?"

"Oh, no."

"Pineapple."

"Gag me with a knife."

"What do you want then, fair Piper? I don't think they have a red velvet pizza."

"That doesn't sound half bad, to be honest." She grinned. "But seriously, what about pepperoni with onions and some chicken wings?"

"That sounds good to me. Do you have any beer?"

"No."

"Vodka?"

"No."

"Whiskey?"

"No."

"Gin?"

"Are you serious?" She laughed. "Do I look like the sort of woman who drinks gin?"

"I've heard that plenty of women love a stiff gin and tonic."

"Plenty of women that aren't me." She made a face. "I like sweet cocktails and red wine."

"Fine, I'll have some red wine." I sighed. "Better than nothing, I suppose."

"Oh, I don't *have* any red wine." She laughed. "I was just saying I like it."

"What alcohol do you have Piper ... what's your last name?"

"What do you care?"

"You know mine."

"Well, not really." She looked thoughtful. "I know your stage name is Oracle Lion and I know your real first name is

Zach, but I have a feeling your real last name isn't Lion, is it?"

"I'm a lion, hear me roar." I faked a roar and laughed as she rolled her eyes. "It's Houston."

"Zach Houston?" She smiled then. "I like that. It's smooth."

"So who are you, Piper?"

"I am Piper Pig and I go oink, oink, oink." She giggled and my stomach flipped a little bit at the sound. "No, but seriously, my last name is Meadows. I'm Piper Meadows."

"Phew, for a second I thought you were going to say your last name was Fox."

"Why did you think that?"

"I thought you were going to ask me, what does the fox say?"

"Oh, Zach," she groaned. "I can't believe you're an A list star?"

"Why?" I pumped my bicep. "Do I look more like an X list star?"

"X list star?"

"XXX, baby." I felt giddy as I joked around with Piper. It had been a long time since I'd felt this comfortable being myself and I liked it. I missed being carefree and not having to watch every little thing that I said. "Though wasn't there that *Fast and Furious* movie that was called XXX? I always thought that was a stupid name."

"I haven't watched any *Fast and Furious* movies in ages." She shook her head. "I have no idea. I don't watch that many movies, to be honest, at least not at the movie theater. They're so expensive."

"Yet you still watched the *Babymaker* movies?" I did a little dance. "I'm honored."

"You should be." She laughed and shook her hair around. I watched the curls bounce across her shoulder and wondered what her strands would feel like moving across my face and chest as she rode me. I kept that thought to myself, though. I didn't want to give her a reason to start becoming bitchy again. Also, I knew I wanted her badly and I was pretty confident she wanted me as well. I just had to play it slowly. I had a feeling that by the end of the night, all of our dreams would come true.

CHAPTER 6

PIPER

I'D NEVER SPENT TOO much time wondering what it would feel like to hang out with someone famous, but if I had, I never would have thought that it would have felt so normal. Zach, as I'd already come to think of him, was much more normal and down to earth than I would have ever thought. It helped that he had turned out to be the weird-but-funny guy I'd met in the cupcake store earlier. In a matter of a few hours, I'd gone from wanting to slap Oracle Lion's face to wanting to kiss Zach Houston's. It certainly didn't hurt that he was sitting so close to me that I could feel the heat emanating from his body on my skin. My arm hairs were on high alert and every part of my body loved it when he accidentally touched me or got too close.

"These are some darn good wings." Zach said as he reached for another wing eagerly. "The pizza isn't so great, but the wings!"

"Don't you be dissing on my pizza," I growled at him as I

took another slice. I had to admit to myself it wasn't the best pizza I'd ever had in my life, but I wasn't going to say that out loud. "But I do agree the wings are good."

"You have a little sauce on your face." His eyes twinkled as he stared at me. I swallowed hard.

"Oh? Where?" I reached up to wipe my face, but he just shook his head.

"Wrong spot."

"Where is it?" I said as I reached my hand to the other side of my face.

"Nope."

"Then where?"

"Higher, to the right, wait ...

He and leaned forward, and before I knew what was happening, he was right next to me and his tongue was licking sauce from the side of my mouth firmly and sensually. His tongue then licked my bottom lip for a second and I froze. Was he going to kiss me as well? But he just moved back and grinned.

"I figured I'd help you out. Turns out the sauce tastes even better when it's coming off of your lips." He licked his lips slowly, and my whole body shuddered as it imagined feeling his tongue all over me, in places that hadn't felt the touch of a tongue or anything else in what felt like forever.

"Oh." I sounded like an idiot, but I didn't know what else to say. Part of me wanted to tell him off, but another part wanted to tell him not to stop. I felt so comfortable with him, which was surprising considering how I'd run away from him in the club. "So are we going to watch something or whatever ..."

My voice trailed off. It was past midnight now. Maybe he wanted to head home or something.

"What does 'or whatever' consist of? There are many things that I'd love to be doing."

"You wish." I giggled and jumped up off of the couch to carry my plate to the kitchen and to cool myself down. I need a couple of moments to myself to level my breathing and figure out where I wanted the night to go.

It was quite obvious to me that if I wanted to have sex with Zach, then I could, but then it also hit me that this would definitely be a one-night stand and I just wasn't sure if that was what I wanted. And wasn't he dating some model or something? I could have sworn I'd read something about him and some model recently. I wanted to bring it up, but then I wasn't sure if that would be overstepping the mark? Did I have any reason to ask him? I mean, it wasn't like this was going to be anything. He was a movie star, and he seemed to date a new girl every week. Maybe I should just go with the flow? What harm could one night of fun do? I wondered if I would regret saying no.

"So you and Alexa are just in town for the weekend?" Zach spoke behind me, and I turned around in surprise to see that he had followed me towards the kitchen. "And then back to North Cal?"

"Yup." I nodded as I took his plate and put it into the sink and ran hot water over it for two seconds. "We just came to have a fun weekend."

"And she left you ..."

"Well, I'm sure she's having fun." I shrugged and looked up into his eyes. He looked mischievous and larger than life standing there in the doorway. I swallowed hard as he took a step towards me.

"So was that the plan?"

"Was what the plan?" I took a step back into the cupboards behind me as he took a step towards me.

"Did you guys want to snag two stars to hook up with for the weekend before you went back to your boring housewife lives?"

"Uhm, we're not married, so neither one of us are house-wives. We're don't have boring lives, either." The last part was a bit of a lie. My life was fairly boring. "And no, we didn't come to LA to hook up with two stars. We didn't come to LA to hook up at all."

"So, your wildest dreams came true, then?"

"What wildest dreams?" I made a face at him and I could feel my breathing increasing as he took a closer step towards me.

"Of me."

"I've never had dreams of you."

"You've never had dreams of me being your baby daddy?" He said in a husky voice. The same voice he used in the *Baby-maker* movies.

He gave me his signature smile, and it took everything in me to not drop to my knees, unzip his pants and take his manhood out. I had a strong urge to bring him to his knees figuratively. I wanted to see his eyes rolling back in his head as he begged me not to stop. I could feel my face growing warm. It wasn't every day that I wanted to give a blowjob to a man I barely knew, but Zach was so hot and I was so attracted to him. I was pretty sure I could feel the sweat drip-ping down my body.

"Not really. How many kids do you have in those movies now? Twenty?" I joked around about his popular franchise, but I didn't want to think about what we'd have to do for him to become my baby daddy. Not that he was offering to have a baby with me. I knew he wasn't trying to commit to any sort of future with me.

"Five." He said taking another step towards me. "The movies are the gift that keeps on giving. Each new movie has to include a new baby."

"And more drama in the house." I laughed.

The *Babymaker* movies were about a rigid army ranger

who never wanted to get married and then he meets a nurse and has a fling and she becomes pregnant. He tries to deny that the kid is his, but then, because this was Hollywood, he realizes how much he loves the nurse and the baby and proposes to her. They end up getting married, and basically each movie was about them having one more kid and more drama in their lives. The movies were cheesy and over-the-top, but they made millions at the box office. In fact, they had turned Oracle Lion into a household name and the subject of many women's dreams. It didn't hurt that he had his shirt off in most of each movie, and let's just say that I could picture him with his shirt off right now as he stood in front of me. I was curious to see if the abs he had in the movie were the abs he had in real life.

"So do you really have a six-pack?" I said out loud, completely mortifying myself. Why had I said that? Oh, right, I'd had too much alcohol.

"Sorry, what did you say?" He looked surprised, but there was a light in his eye that I hadn't seen before.

"I said, every new baby you have results in more drama in your house in the *Babymaker* movies and that you need a six-pack to uhm ..." The words stumbled out of mouth. "You need a six-pack to cope."

"A six-pack to cope?" He chuckled, his head tilted back, but his eyes were still on mine. "Hmmm."

"Hmmm what?" I said, wondering if he'd bought my dreadful coverup.

"Does this answer your question?" Slowly, he lifted up his shirt and showed me his toned and muscular abs, and let me just say I think he had an eight-pack. My mouth went dry and I couldn't even formulate a sentence as I stared at his tan, perfectly smooth chest. I wondered if he shaved or waxed. Not that I cared. My fingers itched to creep forward and trace the lines in his stomach. Never had I seen a more perfect male specimen than I was looking at now, and I hadn't even seen him naked.

I flushed at the thought of seeing his entire body. The biggest question in my mind was if he was well-endowed. It would be unfair to other men in the world if Zach was not just incredibly good looking but had a big cock as well. I suddenly I felt like that was my mission for the night: find out how blessed or unblessed Zach was. Would he live up to his 'lion' name?

I started giggling, and when I looked into Zach's eyes, he had a puzzled look on his face.

"Is my chest funny?"

He took another step towards me. If he took one more step, he would practically be on top of me. Not that I was sure I would complain. I giggled one more time, and he grabbed my hands.

"Piper Meadows, what is so funny?"

"Nothing." I shook my head. "I can't sleep with you." I pulled my hands out of him and touched his chest. I wanted to push them up under his shirt and touch his bare skin, but I wasn't that brazen.

"Sleep with me?" He raised an eyebrow and his lips started twitching. "Is that because you think I snore?"

"Snore?" I blinked at him, my hand still touching his chest.

"I don't snore loudly."

"Huh?"

"You said you can't sleep with me, and I was wondering if that was because you think I snore and will wake you up?"

His voice was so smooth that I nearly didn't notice it when he grabbed my hand and put it under his shirt and on his warm silky skin. His stomach felt taunt and hard beneath my fingers, and I ran my fingers along his ripples. I felt his sharp intake of breath at my touch and I smiled to myself.

"I wasn't talking about *sleep* sleep," I said, way too honestly.

"What were you talking about, then?"

"You know." My face blushed as I ran my fingers up higher to his pecs. His body felt magnificent and I could feel his heart racing under my skin.

"What do I know?" He lowered his voice as he took that final step. He reached over to me and his fingers grazed down my cheek.

"You know," I squeaked out and before I knew what was happening, he was lifting me up and placing me on the countertop. "I can't sit up here," I protested as his hands fell to my legs and he stroked down my thighs. "Zach."

"I like how you say my name," he said as his hands moved to the side and grazed my ass before settling on my waist. "Say it again."

"Zach," I said staring into his deep blue eyes. "Or would you rather I call you Oracle?"

"Nope. I hate the name Oracle." His voice sounded bitter, and I looked up at him in surprise.

"You hate your name?"

"It's not my name, it's my stage name." He shrugged. "It stands out, I suppose. It is what it is."

"Why don't you like it?" I asked him, wanting him to share more with me, wanting to know more about this man who I wanted to sleep with so badly.

"Enough with the questions." He put a finger on my lips. "We're doing too much talking."

"I enjoy talking." I could feel my entire body starting shake slightly from being so close to him. It was like the moments before an earthquake when you feel a little tremble, but you know the big quake is coming soon.

"I still don't even know what you do for a living."

"I'm a writer," I said with a smile.

"What do you write?"

"Articles for *The National Examiner*." He froze for a few seconds before I started laughing. "Got ya! No, I write romance. I used to write historical romance because I studied history in college, but now I'm working on something new."

"Oh?" He looked genuinely interested which surprised me. "What are you working on now?"

"I'd rather not say, to be honest."

"No worries." He nodded, then he gave me one of his wide, handsome smiles. "Okay, so I think we know enough about each other now, we can continue."

"Continue with what?"

"Whatever it was we were doing before we started making small talk." His voice was light and lyrical, but it wasn't his words that had my heart racing. It was his hands moving my shorts up and caressing the inner skin of my thighs that made me want to jump into his arms.

"Zach." I reached up and touched the sides of his face.

He grabbed my left hand and moved it to his lips and kissed it gently. "Yes, Piper?"

"Did we get any dessert?" My heart was thudding as I changed the subject. I wanted him so badly, but it all seemed too soon for me.

"I can be your dessert," he said in a husky voice, and before I knew what was happening, he was kissing me, warm and hard.

He pushed his way in between my legs and pulled me towards him. I wrapped my arms around his neck and kissed him back, my legs trembling as he slid his tongue into my mouth. It tasted like crisp juicy apples, and I sucked on it for a second before he started nibbling on my bottom lip. I moaned against his mouth as he slipped a hand inside my shorts and rubbed against the top of my panties. Instinctively, I closed my legs around his fingers. He grunted as he felt my wetness, which turned me on even more and I kissed him harder. He lifted me up off of the countertop and I wrapped my legs around his waist. I was self-conscious for all of two seconds, worried that I would be too heavy for him to hold up, but then I shrugged it off. He was a strong man with huge muscles; if he couldn't hold me up then something was wrong with him, not me.

"You taste so good." He walked me towards the living room and then stopped and pulled away from me slightly. "Where's the bedroom?"

I pointed to the far corner, and he carried me easily towards the bedroom. I ran my hands through his silky hair and sighed happily.

"You're just as hot as I thought you'd be," I whispered into his ear, and he laughed.

"So you're now fully admitting you know who I am and that you've had fantasies about me?"

"I've never had a fantasy about you."

"You mean you've never pictured my face when you've been fucking another guy? You've never thought to yourself, what would I do for one night with Oracle Lion?"

He placed me down on the bed as we entered the bedroom and promptly lay down next to me. His hands slid under my t-shirt and up to my breasts. His fingers quickly found my nipples, and then he rolled them across his palms. I moaned as he started kissing the side of my face at the same time, and I reached over and touched his chest under his shirt.

"Shh!" I rolled over and straddled him. "Take your shirt off," I ordered as I reached down to undo the buttons of his shirt. I could feel his hardness underneath me, and I deliberately rocked back and forth on top of him as I peeled his shirt open. His hands grabbed ahold of my waist and held me still for a few seconds and he gazed up at me with an expression I couldn't quite read.

"You're a bossy one, huh?" He shook his head slightly. "I wouldn't have guessed you'd be so take-charge."

"Why? Did you want to be the one to boss me around? Do you want me to get down on my knees so you can spank me and take me from behind?" I bit down on my lower lip as I teased him and rubbed myself on him again.

"I think you watch too much porn." He laughed as he pulled my T-shirt off and rolled me onto my back before quickly disposing of the rest of my clothes. "But I can take charge if that's what you want me to do."

He held my hands up above my head and stared down at my naked body. I could see his eyes on my face, and then on my breasts, before they moved down to my stomach and then lower. I felt hot and vulnerable as he stared at me. I tried not to worry about how my body compared to the models and actresses he dated. I wasn't stick thin. Instead of a six-pack, I had wide hips and big thighs. I wished I was about thirty pounds lighter, but I still loved my body. He let go of my right wrist and ran his fingers down my body, expertly caressing my skin and making me almost giddy with anticipation.

"It seems to me like you've been waiting for this moment all night," he said with a cocky grin. He chuckled as I moaned in excitement. Then something in my brain clicked and I started to get annoyed. Was he really this full of himself?

"It seems to me like you've been waiting all night to get into my bed." I reached up and pushed him over onto his back. My hands fell to his pants and I undid his belt buckle, unzipped his pants, and slid them off, along with his boxer shorts. His cock sprang free and it was even more glorious than I'd expected it to be. Now I knew why he was so cocky, but just because he was big didn't mean he knew what to do with it.

"What are you going to do next?" He was breathing hard now as he lay flat on his back and looked up at me with a dark expression as I ran my fingers over the tip of his cock.

"What do you want me to do?" I licked my lips and looked down at him. For a few seconds, I could feel every part of my body screaming at me for what I was about to do. This was a once in a lifetime opportunity. I mean, how many movie stars was I going to meet? And then how many would want to sleep with me? "Doesn't even matter, Piper," I chided myself under my breath. Yes, I wanted to sleep with Zach, but ...

"What did you say?" He was practically drooling in anticipation.

"I think I'm feeling tired," I mumbled. I rolled off of him and back down on the bed.

"You what?" he croaked out, and I hid a smile.

"I'm feeling tired, and well, I'm not sure this is a good idea, you know?"

"You what?" he said again like he was in repeat.

"Oracle Lion, you are a huge movie star, and I'm sure many women would love to be in my position. Actually, I know many women have been in my position, but I'm just not feeling it right now." I smiled sweetly and reached down to grab my T-shirt. "So I don't think it's going to be happening between us."

"Are you joking?" He moved over onto his side, the look of shock on his face almost pitiful. "You want me as badly as I want you."

"I'm not going to lie, you're hot and you're a good kisser, but I just don't think this is a good idea, and I always have to trust my gut."

"Well, I wouldn't tell you to not trust your gut." He groaned and lay back on the bed. "Piper Meadows, I do believe you teased me on purpose."

J. S. COOPER

"I didn't," I said, suddenly serious because I hated teases. I turned over to look at him and I touched his chest lightly. "A part of me did and still does want to sleep with you, but it's just not what I want."

"Why not?"

"Honestly?" I asked him and he nodded.

"I don't even know you. I mean, not in the way I pretended earlier not to know who you were, but in a real-life way. I don't know you, and while that doesn't matter to some people, it matters to me and well, you're also ..." I stopped talking then because I didn't want to be completely bitchy.

"I'm also what?" He peered at me curiously.

"You're also a bit of a pompous asshole. Your head, and no, not the head of your cock, is too big. I don't need to make it bigger."

"But you already made it big." He grinned and looked down towards his cock. "See?"

"Zach."

"Yes?" He looked at me hopefully. "Are you changing your mind?"

"No, I'm not changing my mind." I shook my head. "You can leave if you want to."

"You think I want to leave right now because you're not going to have sex with me?" He started playing with my hair, and I nodded gently. "I'm not that sort of guy." He said looking at my face intently. "I mean you're right. You don't know me, and this is a one-night thing, but I wouldn't fuck you and then just roll out of bed and leave."

"Oh, would you buy me breakfast in the morning?"

"If that's what you want, then it would be my pleasure," he said with a smile.

"And then after that?"

"After that what?"

68

"Exactly. After that, we'd go our separate ways our bellies full of pancakes and eggs, and that would be that."

"I take it you don't have many one-night stands," he said with a bemused smile.

"No," I admitted. "I don't have to ask you that question."

"You think you know so much about me, don't you?" He studied my face and sighed. "You can't believe everything you read about in the tabloids."

"So why don't you tell me more about yourself, then?"

"What is this? Are you becoming my therapist instead of my lover?"

"I'm not a therapist. I'm just a history lover who writes romance books, and I leave town tomorrow night, so you don't have to worry about me wanting anything more than that."

"I don't have any deep dark secrets." He wrapped a hand around my waist and rested his palm on my ass, then squeezed it. "You have a very juicy butt. I was looking forward to seeing it bounce up and down on my cock."

"How would you have seen my ass?" I rolled my eyes, but I still blushed.

"Reverse cowgirl." He kissed the side of my face and then he tugged on my earlobe. "And while you were bouncing up and down on me, I would have lifted you off and then entered you from behind, doggy style, so you could feel every single inch of me inside of you. And when you went back to North California tomorrow evening, you'd be wishing that you lived in LA so you could ride me one more time."

"Zach, I ..." My voice drifted off as he blew into my ear and his fingers slid in-between my legs and started rubbing my clit.

"You're so wet for me," he growled and then he pulled away from me and lay back. I almost cried out for him to touch me again, but instead I just lay there, wondering what had happened for him to completely pull away from me. It was silent in the room for a few minutes while I stared at the ceiling, feeling incredibly uncomfortable.

"We should put some clothes on," he blurted out.

I peeked over at him, surprised to see a warm smile on his face instead of an angry look. "I'm super horny right now and I think it will be hard to stop myself if I lie here with you naked."

"I have a top on," I said, and he just laughed as he jumped up and started putting his clothes back on. "Are you leaving?"

"It's late and I should leave, but no." He shook his head. "I thought perhaps you could tell me a bit about your book."

"Oh." I made a face. "Really?"

"You're a writer. I'm a famous actor. Shouldn't you be jumping for this opportunity?"

"I'm not a screenwriter, though, and I don't write films."

"But we can turn any book into a movie." He stopped then and gave me a look. "You're really not from LA, are you? The vultures out there would die for an interaction like this."

"I don't know who you're hooking up with, but not all of us women are just looking to advance our careers you know. Some of us just like to have a good time." I rolled off of the bed and bent down to grab my shorts and pull them on.

"You're different, aren't you?" Zach's eyes were bright as he walked towards me. "I don't know that I've met someone like you."

"What, someone that doesn't want to sleep with you immediately?" I laughed and grabbed his hand impulsively. "I have an idea. Let's go to the beach."

"The beach?" He looked confused. "It's nighttime."

"I like the ocean, and I love the waves," I said. "We can take a walk along the sand and maybe even go for a swim."

"Well, I'm going to have to say no to the swim. We've

both had too much alcohol, but maybe a walk would be nice."
He nodded. "Yeah, let's do it."

"Well, only if you like the beach," I said hesitantly.

"I love the beach," he said with a grin.

"So then, why the hesitation?"

"Going to the beach during the day is a sure-fire way to get accosted by fans. People don't follow the same protocol outdoors like they do in the club. Everyone in the club wants to be cool, so most of them never bother you. Outside, it's a completely different thing."

"Oh, so you were worried you'd be recognized."

"Something like that, but it's night, and I'm sure we won't see anyone."

"Are you worried about fans or paparazzi?" I asked him as I suddenly realized that he most probably wouldn't want to be photographed with the likes of me. I mean, I was a no one. He was only ever pictured with Victoria's Secret Models and leggy actresses.

"Neither. Come on, let's go."

"But how will we get there? We can't drive."

"Well, I think we're about a ten-minute walk to Santa Monica Pier. I think we'll make it." He grinned and squeezed my hand. "Come on, lazybones."

"I'm not lazy," I lied. I had kinda wanted him to suggest getting an Uber there, even though it was only ten-minute walk away. And that was why I still had the belly I'd wanted to lose for years. "Come on then. Let's walk, but only if you tell me more about yourself. I want to know everything about you, Zach Houston."

CHAPTER 7

Oracle

Piper ran into the water, her hair flowing behind her in the wind like some sort of siren. She bent down and dipped her fingers into the water and then she turned towards me. "Aren't you going to dip your feet in the water?" she called.

"I bet it's freezing!" I shouted as I walked towards her slowly, the hardness in my pants wanting to burst out of the zipper that enclosed it. I wasn't even sure what I was doing here with her, walking along the beach like we were star-crossed lovers. I think it was because she'd assumed I wanted to leave after she'd played her little game of turning me on and then saying she wanted to stop. I'd wanted to bloody leave. I fucking had blue balls from the way she'd been rubbing up and down on me and then had just left me hanging, but I'd stayed. I wasn't sure why I'd stayed.

That was a lie. I knew why. I stayed because I hadn't wanted to confirm her negative opinion of me. At the club, she'd thought I was a jerk from the get-go, and I didn't want to give her reason to go back to those thoughts—if they'd ever left her.

"Come on, Zach!" She ran back towards me, and I could see that she was shivering slightly in the cool night air. I pulled her into my arms as she got closer to me and I rubbed her shoulders. "Don't you want to feel the water?" She gazed up at me with wide brown eyes and gave me a small smile. "I mean, I think when we left the apartment I said I wanted to hear about you, but we spent the whole walk here talking about how much I want to get a dog."

"You don't want to know about me, I'm a very boring person."

"I think you're far from boring." Her arms wrapped around my waist and she rested her head on my chest.

"I'm the most boring man you'll ever meet." I stared at the sky for a few seconds. "Look up there." I pointed to the sky. "See those stars?" I drew a line in the sky. "That's the Draco constellation."

"Oh, is it?" She looked up at the sky and I could see her trying to follow my finger.

"Or ... maybe not," I said as I saw one of the stars moving. It was actually an airplane. "I thought it was the Draco."

"I didn't know you were into astronomy."

"I'm not." I realized I'd fucked up. "I had a friend when I was younger that used to love to stargaze in Florida. I don't really know much."

"Oh?"

She looked like she wanted to ask me more, so I grabbed her hand and tugged it. "Come on then, let's go sample the water."

"Sample the water? Are we tasting it?"

"No," I laughed, let go of her hand, and started to run. "Race ya! The first one to the water wins!"

"No fair, you started running before me!"

I heard her gasping as she ran towards the shoreline with me. I reached the edge of the water and quickly pulled off my shoes, rolled up my pants and dipped my feet into the ocean.

I quickly took a few steps back. "It's bloody freezing in there."

"It *is* the Pacific." She grinned as she joined me and then started flicking me with water. I leaned down and splashed her with water and she shrieked as I drenched her.

"I've always preferred the Atlantic. So much warmer."

"Oh, yeah?" She stopped splashing me and stood there for a few seconds. "Have you spent a lot of time there?"

"Yeah. I grew up in Florida, but I think you knew that already."

"Kinda." She admitted in a soft voice. "Orlando, right? You and Jackson grew up together?"

"Yes, Jackson and I grew up together. We've been best friends since we were eight." I smiled as I thought of Jackson as a young boy. "We went to school together and actually lived on the same street, but not in Orlando."

"In Florida, though?"

"You sure you're not a reporter?" I laughed, but I was half-serious. I found it hard to trust new people and didn't like opening up. "But yes, in Florida, in a small town called Palm Bay."

"Sounds cool."

"It was okay." I shrugged. "Nothing special, but we were close to the beach." I paused for a few seconds. "We used to spend every weekend at Indialantic beach and sometimes we'd go down to Stuart. A lot of the pro surfers used to practice there, and we had a friend that was hoping to go pro." I looked at her face and could see that she was listening to me intently. "Actually, the same friend that liked looking at the stars," I said and I wanted to kick myself. I was revealing too much.

"Did you surf as well, then?" she asked, and I was grateful that she was taking the conversation in a different direction.

"I tried, but I was never a natural. Jackson and I, well, we were always artsier. You know, he started playing the guitar when he was four. He was a natural."

"I've heard something like that." She nodded. "Were you in drama in school?"

"You'd think so, right?" I laughed as I shook my head. "But no, I focused a lot on classes. I was in dual enrollment classes at the local community college, Brevard Community College." I thought back to my high school days. How long ago they seemed now. "And I had a job to help my mom pay the rent."

"Oh?" She sounded surprised. "Where did you work?"

"Papa Johns." I smiled. "Maybe that's why I love pizza so much."

"Were your parents divorced?" she asked softly and I felt my heart hardening as I thought about my parents' marriage and my early childhood.

"Something like that." I nodded and then grabbed her arms and pulled her towards me. "Too many serious questions have been asked. Can I kiss you?"

She looked like she wanted to ask me something else, but I think she could tell from my tone that I was done answering questions.

"If we kiss, it might lead to something more," she said, tipping her head back. The moonlight illuminated her face, and when she looked back at me, she reminded me of a beautiful nymph, ready to captivate me and make me hers.

"Would that be so bad?" I asked her softly. I pulled her into me so that she could feel my hardness against her stomach. "I know this isn't something you normally do, but what's the harm? I want you very badly, Piper Meadows. I want to please you. I want to pleasure you. I want to show you that I ..."

My voice trailed off as she took a step away from me. She slid her hands out of mine, and my jaw dropped as I watched her slowly pull her off first her top and then her shorts. She stood there in front of me, naked, and I'd never been more turned on in my life.

"What are you doing?" I asked her as she started to dance in front of me, her body sensual and glowing in the moonlight. "You are a nymph, aren't you?"

"I'm just a love machine," she sang as she danced and then she raised her hands in the air and turned around swaying like a belly dancer. My eyes could not leave her body and I moved towards her with some sort of magnetic attraction. I was drawn to this woman like a moth to a flame.

"You're driving me crazy, woman."

"How crazy?"

"This crazy." I grabbed her around the waist and pulled her towards me. "Are you trying to bewitch me?" I whispered against her lips as she pressed herself into me and batted her eyelashes.

"I don't think anyone can bewitch you, Oracle Lion, aka Zach Houston." Her voice was sexy and seductive and her words mesmerized me. "If anything, you're the one bewitching me."

"How much have you had to drink, Piper?" I held her close to me. "I think I should get you home."

"Don't you want me?" She grinned as she leaned up to kiss me.

"Of course I want you, but I don't think this is the place."

"I didn't think there was a place you would say no."

"Oh, and why is that?"

"You seem to be with a different woman every other week."

"Oh?"

"I mean, weren't you just dating that one model, what was her name, Cassie Cash?"

"Cassie and I never dated."

"Oh, okay, did you just have sex, then?"

"Contrary to what you think you know, we never had sex, either."

"What?" She paused then and I could see her thinking as she gazed up at me. "But what sort of relationship is that?"

"Exactly, there was no relationship. Everything you read in the tabloids isn't true, you know, Piper. I'm not Cassanova."

"So you don't get around?"

"Well, I didn't say that." I laughed and bent down and picked up her clothes. "Here, put these on and let me take you home. I think the fresh air, water, and alcohol have all gone to your head."

"But I want to make love."

"As do I, but not if you're drunk. Let's see how you feel in the morning."

"In the morning?" She blinked at me as she held onto my arm with one hand and put her clothes on with the other hand. "Aren't you going home?"

"No, I think I should spend the night, in case you feel sick and need anything."

"That's why you're staying the night?"

She gave me an impish look that made her look even cuter than before, and I just laughed. It was weird how comfortable I felt with Piper, seeing as I'd never met her before today and I never felt comfortable with anyone. I met a lot of women and a lot of women were into me, but it never felt genuine, not like it did with her. I always wondered if they were into me or if they were into just being with a star. With Piper, that thought never even crossed my mind. I truly believed she was her true self with me. Even if her true self was a bit all over the place.

"Let's get you home."

I squeezed her hand as we made our way off the beach. We strolled lazily along the sand, and Piper started telling me a story about when she and Alexa had gone to what they thought was a regular dance club in San Francisco but had turned out to be a bondage club. She was open and free and I listened to her story, chuckling and turned on.

Part of me couldn't believe that I'd turned down sex on the beach, but I knew I wouldn't have been happy with myself if I'd let it happen. I wanted Piper to want me when she was completely sober as well. And I was willing to wait until morning for that to happen.

CHAPTER 8

PIPER

THE SOUND of light snoring woke me up.

I opened my eyes feeling slightly confused as to where the sound was coming from. Then I froze as I saw the golden blond hairs on the tan chest directly next to my face. I glanced up and saw the handsome face of a sleeping Zach Houston.

Daaammn, had I slept with him?

I reached down to see if I had my panties on, and when I felt the lacy material, I had to admit I was slightly disappointed. As I lay there, memories of the previous night flashed into my mind. I couldn't stop myself groaning out loud as I remembered my little naked dance on the beach.

And this was why I didn't normally drink on an empty stomach.

I'd had pizza later in the night, but obviously that had been too late to combat the evils of alcohol. I was grateful that I wasn't feeling hungover, though, and that I was sober enough to appreciate his naked chest and the morning stubble that grew on his face.

"What's the groan for?"

Zach gave me a wide smile as his eyes opened. There was a naughty twinkle in them, and I wondered if he'd been awake before me. But no, that wasn't possible, he'd been snoring, hadn't he? I stilled for a few moments as I realized that the snoring that had woken me might have been my own. I groaned again, thinking that this morning couldn't possibly be any more embarrassing.

"My snoring," I said before I could stop myself. I blushed slightly at his grin as he basically confirmed that it had been me after all. "Did I wake you up?"

"Yes, but not because of your snoring."

"Oh?" I moved over slightly so that I could look at his face properly without straining my neck and wondered if I should move off of him.

"Your hand got me excited." He winked, and I instinctively moved my hands to see what he was talking about.

My right hand felt numb as I was lying on top of it, but as I moved my left hand, I realized it was placed lightly on his cock. I could feel it growing hard as I moved my hand back and forth.

"And it's continuing to get me excited."

"Oh, uh, sorry." I pulled my hand away, and he chuckled. I looked back into his smiling blue eyes and blinked rapidly, trying to wake myself from what had to be a dream.

"Have you got something in your eyes?" His voice was caring and I stopped blinking. "Also, how are you feeling this morning?"

"Nothing in my eyes, and fine. Why?"

"You seemed like you had quite a bit to drink last night when you were shaking your coconuts on the beach."

Shaking my coconuts on the beach? My face reddened as I

stared at his deadpan expression. I could tell that he was totally thinking about a naked me trying to dance sensually in the night air. Oh God, I remembered asking him to take me. Where was my shame? He most probably thought I was bipolar or something with my ever-changing moods. From goofy in the cupcake store, to standoffish in the club, to wanton once he came back to the apartment, to cold when we going to have sex and then back to wanton on the beach. To be honest, I was surprised he was still here. I was acting like a crazy woman.

"Not that I didn't enjoy it. You're quite the dancer." He grinned, and before I knew what was going on, I felt his hand on my stomach, creeping up under my top. His lips moved to the side of my lips and he kissed me lightly. "In fact, if you'd like to give me another performance right now, I'd be happy to watch."

"Another performance?" I croaked out. Why was he delighting in embarrassing me?

"You know."

His lips found their way to mine. His teeth tugged gently on my lower lip, and then I felt his hand behind my neck, pulling on my hair. My scalp tingled a little bit, but I soon forgot the slight pain as I enjoyed the feel of his lips on mine.

"I want you to dance for me again," he whispered against my lips and then blew gently on my skin.

I swallowed at the intimate gesture and kissed him back lightly. I wanted to grab his hair and pull him against me. I wanted to slide my tongue into his mouth and grab his cock and glide on top of him. Even more than I'd wanted to the night before. I was no longer drunk, but I still wanted him.

The only thing stopping me was the fact that I was pretty sure I had morning breath and smeared mascara, and I didn't want to be all over him when I wasn't at my best. At least let me brush my teeth and wash my face. That wasn't too much for a girl to ask for. I mean, it's not like I was going to get this opportunity again. He was a hot movie star. And yeah, he was a cocky bastard, but what did I care? And I wasn't a mistress or cheater or whatever because he wasn't actually dating Cassie Cash and he never had been. At least, that's what he'd said the night before and I believed him. I mean, maybe they'd had sex, but I'm sure he had a lot of sex with a lot of women. It didn't mean much. Just like him sleeping with me didn't mean much. Well, to him at least.

To me, well to me, it meant a lot. And it wasn't just because he was a movie star. I'd seen a different side to him last night. He'd been caring and sweet and funny and nothing like what I'd thought he'd be like.

"You don't want to?" He pulled away and I could see the hesitancy in his face.

"I do, but ..." My voice trailed off. How did you tell a guy you were nervous you had bad breath? I mean, it wasn't like he was my boyfriend. It just felt awkward.

"But?"

"Can I, well, we, brush our teeth first?" I asked him with a small shrug, loving the feel of his hands on my back. I made sure to keep eye contact because I didn't want him to think I was nervous, even though inside every nerve ending was shaking.

"Are you saying that my breath smells?"

He laughed and then gave me a huge kiss on the lips. I couldn't stop myself from kissing him back, and I had to admit that the last thing I was thinking about as our lips caressed was his breath. His hand cupped my breast as he rolled me over onto my back. Throwing caution to the wind, I grabbed his head and kissed him back hard as my fingers ran through his silky tresses. He nudged my legs open with his knee and then kissed down my neck before pulling my top off in what felt like nanoseconds.

"So beautiful," he murmured as he kissed down the valley between my breasts and then towards my stomach. I felt his hands on my breasts playing with my nipples and my body was in overdrive with pleasure. His fingers flicked my nipples as his mouth kept heading lower. I closed my eyes and let my body submit to him and whatever he wanted to do. My fingers played with his hair and I heard him chuckle as my body froze still when his lips kissed me in between my legs over my shorts.

"Zach ..." I moaned as I felt his fingers on the top of my shorts nudging them down. "Are you ..." I stopped talking because my tongue would no longer work. My shorts were now off and he was kissing up the side of my calf and towards my thighs. His lips alternated with his tongue on my skin as he made his way up my legs and I waited in barely conscious anticipation to feel his lips on my sweet spot.

"You taste like the ocean," he growled against my inner thigh and his eyes glanced up at mine. "That salty-sweet taste is my favorite."

"Oh?" I reached down and grabbed his hair again, wanting to push his head in between my legs.

"I love the ocean," he said. "Especially fishing." He winked and then his tongue lightly licked my clit and my entire body trembled as if an earthquake had just passed through the room. Then he started sucking, and I didn't know what to do with my hands or my body. Moans flew out of my mouth, but I barely noticed them. All I could feel was the build-up in my stomach and between my legs. His tongue lightly entered me and I could feel the wetness seeping out of me.

With a grunt, he lifted my legs up and over his shoulders and buried his face between my legs, licking and sucking for what felt like forever. Then he moved back up and kissed me on the mouth, sliding his boxers off with one hand as he kissed me. His other hand touched my breast and played with my nipple as I reached down to touch his cock. It felt huge in my fingers and I pressed myself into him. His body was warm and hard next to me, and I kissed him hard.

My fingers moved up and down his shaft and then played with the increasingly moist head of his cock. He muttered something against my lips as I reached further down and squeezed his balls. I could feel him shaking against me as I made a circle with my thumb and finger and ran it tightly back up his cock. I pushed him ,, so that he was lying on his back and kissed his lips one last time before making my way down his chest.

I lightly sucked his nipples and then kissed down to his stomach. I stared at his abs for a few seconds and then looked further down. His cock stood to attention, and while I wasn't great with numbers it looked like it had to be at least 7 or 8 inches long and incredibly thick; not too thick, though, the girth was just about perfect. To be fair, Zach Houston had the most gorgeous penis I'd ever seen. And it went without saying that he was the most well-endowed man I'd ever been with—a part of me wondered if he'd be able to fit all the way. I continued kissing down his stomach, and then because I could help myself, I took the tip of his cock in my mouth.

"Oh, shit," he groaned and I felt his hands in my hair.

The sound of his voice turned me on and encouraged me to keep going. I took more of his cock into my mouth and sucked it long and hard, taking it as deep as I could. He seemed to be growing even bigger as I sucked, and I felt him pulling on my hair harder as his breathing grew faster and faster.

"Stop," he groaned a few minutes later. "I'm going to blow."

"I don't mind," I said with a small smile as I could feel his body start to shudder.

"I want to come in your other lips," he answered, his voice deep and husky. The dirtiness of his words made me come slightly.

"Hold on."

He rolled over and reached into his pants pocket again and I watched as he pulled out a strip of condoms. He ripped open a packet and pulled a condom out, and before I knew what was happening, he was slipping it onto his hard cock. He grabbed my hands and pulled me up and then pushed me slightly so that I was on my back.

"First position will be traditional and then we can go crazy," he said with another wink and I felt the tip of his cock at my opening. His fingers rubbed my clit and he groaned. "You're so wet for me." He kissed me passionately, his tongue slipping into my mouth at the same time his cock entered me, hard and deep.

I bit down on his lip in shock and pleasure as I felt him inside of me deeper than I'd ever felt someone before. His finger was still rubbing my clit and all my senses were over-whelmed with the pleasure he was giving me.

"Faster," I moaned, barely able to keep up as I flexed my muscles in rhythm to his grinding.

"Say my name," he said as I started writhing beneath him more urgently.

"Go faster," I panted, feeling my release close, but not wanting to say his name for some reason. "Please," I groaned as he pulled out of me completely and stared down at me. "Zach, please."

"Please what?" He gave me a wicked grin, and I bit down on my lower lip as he rubbed the tip of his cock against my clit. I was about ready to burst, but I needed to feel him inside of me.

"Zach Houston, please fuck me harder." My fingernails dug into his back and I bit down on his shoulder. "*Now*."

He chuckled for two seconds before entering me again. This time he moved harder and faster than I had ever thought possible, and I moved along with him, trying to keep up. I felt the pressure building up so that I couldn't stop it and I screamed when I felt myself coming long and hard. He stared down at me with a satisfied smile and then increased his pace faster, grabbing my hips and slamming into me with abandon.

"Fuck, yes," he grunted.

He slammed into me two more times before he paused and came inside of me. He kissed my neck as he lay next to me, then a few seconds later than he pulled out of me, took the condom off, and placed it on the side table next to the bed. He kissed me on the lips and looked into my eyes and smiled.

"That was worth the wait, Piper Meadows. That was definitely worth the wait."

"Worth the wait?" I laughed. "We only met yesterday. What wait are you talking about?"

Normally, I would have felt slightly embarrassed or guilty about having slept with a man I'd just met, but in this moment I didn't care at all. This had been the best sex of my life so far, and it *had* been well worth it. Plus, it was Oracle Lion—well, Zach Houston—and I was pretty sure I would have regretted missing out. He wasn't as big of an ass as I'd thought.

"You know you wanted me as soon as you saw me at the club." He nodded with a cocky smile. "Our eyes met, and you thought to yourself, I'd love to be riding Oracle Lion tonight. Maybe you were even contemplating lifting up your skirt and taking me to the dance floor." His fingers reached between my legs and rubbed. "Or maybe you were hoping for a three-some with me and Jackson." His lips made their way to my ear. "One of us fucking you while the other one played with your tits."

I stilled at his words and looked at him with an annoyed expression.

"I'm just joking," he laughed and put his hands up in the air. "Don't kill me."

"Uh huh," I mumbled, feeling less happy than I had a few minutes ago. Had he been joking? It didn't sound like it to me. Maybe that had been the plan all along. Maybe they did have threesomes or foursomes or couple swaps or whatever. Maybe they'd thought they'd hit the jackpot when Alexa had arrived looking all hot and sexy.

"Piper, I'm joking." He touched the side of my face and stroked down to my collarbone. "I don't do threesomes, and even if you'd begged me, I would have had to have said no."

"If I had begged you?" I hit him on the shoulder, and he burst out laughing. "Very funny. This isn't something I do often you know. If you think I just sleep around and ..." My voice trailed off as I watched him chuckling to himself. "Are you laughing at me?"

"Would I do that?" He pulled me into his arms. "It's been a nice night, Piper. Well, I should say a nice night and morning. It's been just what I needed."

"Yeah, it has been nice." I snuggled into his arms and closed my eyes. "You've given me some inspiration for my next book," I said with a secret smile and shook my head as his eyes grew inquisitive. "And no, I'm not going to tell you what it's about."

THE BANGING FRONT door awoke me and I stretched against a sleepy Zach who was watching me with hooded eyes. "Oops, I guess I fell asleep."

"I guess you did," he said with a small smile and I wondered what he was thinking.

"I guess Alexa is back," I said stupidly. "I wonder if Jackson is with her. Maybe they want to get brunch or something."

"Hmm."

Before I could say anything else, Alexa was opening my bedroom door and striding in. "You will never believe what I found out about Jackson Camden." She said as she walked in and stopped, her eyes were wide and her hair was wild.

"Score, Piper. I knew you'd get Oracle Lion into the sack one of these days."

Alexa grinned wickedly, though the smile didn't reach her eyes and before Zach and I knew what was happening, she was snapping a photo of us with her phone, flash on and blinding us with its light.

"If times get hard again, this will be worth a pretty penny." She winked at me before heading out of the room again.

I looked over at Zach with a small smile about to apologize for Alexa's poor sense of humor, but all humor and affection had gone from his face. He looked at me stonily and I could feel his emotional and physical withdrawal from me.

"She's just joking." I made to stroke the side of his face, but he recoiled from me. "Zach, are you mad?" My eyes took in the veiled anger in his face. He shook his head and pulled away from me.

"Nope." He looked at his watch in an exaggerated fashion and then reached down to his pants and pulled his phone out of his pocket, swiped a couple of times and appeared to be reading something. He glanced up at me with narrowed eyes and gave me a bitter smile. "Some writer, eh?"

"Excuse me, what?" I stared at him, feeling emptiness already fill me as he jumped up out of the bed.

"I have to go." He pulled on his clothes quickly, typed

something on his phone, and gave me one long last glance. "It's been real. Thanks for the fun," he said as he walked towards the bedroom door. He stopped at the door and looked back at me with disdain, then took a leather wallet out of his pocket, opened it, and pulled out a stack of bills, which he threw onto the bed.

"That's for you," he said with a twist of his lips. Then he moved back towards the bed and stared down at a shocked me. "And if I see that photo of us in any tabloids, I will sue you for every penny you have." And with that, he was gone. I sat on the bed in shock, wondering what the hell had just happened. He couldn't have been that upset because of Alexa's joke, could he? Granted, it had been in poor taste, but it had just been a joke.

"What the hell happened to Oracle?" Alexa walked into the room looking confused. "He just stormed out of the apartment and gave me the dirtiest look I've ever been given in my life."

"Girl, I have no idea." I shook my head. "But I knew he was an asshole." I sighed as I picked up the stack of bills he'd left on the bed. "He basically just called me a whore."

"What? Alexa's jaw dropped. "No way."

"He dropped all these bills on the bed." I counted them quickly. "Two thousand dollars." I held the money up in shock. "He left two thousand dollars."

"Did he think you were a prostitute?" Alexa sat on the side of the bed and gave me a look. "How rude."

"I don't think he did." I shook my head slightly and then pointed at her. "He got all funny when you took that photo. Why did you take that photo?" It was then that I noticed that Alexa looked upset with red eyes. "Have you been crying?"

"You won't believe what happened." She said collapsing down on the bed. "Ugh, I hate men."

"Does this have to do with what you said you found out about Jackson Camden?" I thought back to her words when she entered the room.

"Yes." She nodded. "You're not going to believe what I found out."

CHAPTER 9

ORACLE

IDIOT!

That's what I was thinking as I walked towards the beach after leaving Piper's place. *Idiot!* I couldn't believe that I'd been taken in by Piper so convincingly. As soon as Alexa had walked into the apartment, I knew something had been off. Jackson was the sort of guy who would have taken her to breakfast and then to lunch and then most probably would have seen if she'd be up for a quickie at the airport before he left.

I'd seen the look on Alexa's face when she'd walked into the bedroom. She hadn't looked happy. Which lead me to believe her night with Jackson hadn't gone as planned. And what was that she'd said about finding some secret out about Jackson?

I looked back down at the text that Jackson had sent me that morning, "Dude, if you're still with that chick, get out of there. I'm pretty sure she and Alexa are journalists and last night was a set-up."

I clenched my fists as I reread his words. No wonder Piper hadn't wanted to tell me what she was working on now. It was a frigging article about me and maybe Jackson. She'd well and truly fooled me. I stared at the photo of the newspaper that Jackson had sent with the text and my heart froze. I sighed as I realized I couldn't go to my private home in Venice beach. I had to go back to the main house and talk with Jackson, and we had to figure out exactly what each one of us had told the girls. And exactly what Alexa had found out.

My mind flashed back to Piper's shocked expression as I'd thrown the money on the bed. She'd looked taken aback and hurt and I bet she was shocked that I'd figured out her secret. I had to give it to her, she'd had me well and truly fooled.

"SHE THOUGHT SHE WAS SO SMART," Jackson growled and slammed the paper down on my dining room table with a loud bang. "She didn't even ask me anything about it, just sat there reading."

"She sat there reading it right in front of you?" I asked him, choosing my words slowly. I could tell from the way he was talking that he was worried. "Did you ask her where she got the paper?"

"I didn't want her to think I was interested or had noticed what she was reading. I didn't want to make her think I knew anything."

"So it could have been a coincidence?" I asked, but really, how could it have been?

"Do I think it's a coincidence that she was reading the *Orlando Sentinel* and the front story was about the reopening of a case from twelve years ago?" He gave me a look that told me he thought I was stupid. "We're in Los Angeles, Zach. Does that sound like a coincidence to you?"

"Did you know?" I didn't even have to ask him the full question. He knew what I was talking about, but I decided to clarify anyway. "Did you know they were reopening the case?"

"I had no idea." He shook his head, his eyes downcast. "I have to call Margaret." Margaret was his younger sister and the only woman that Jackson had truly cared about in his life. "Maybe she knows something."

"But what if she doesn't?" I said softly, touching his shoulder. "Let's just see what happens. You don't want to get her upset or anything."

"Did you say anything to ... what was her name?" he asked me, his eyes searching mine and I could see him relaxing as I shook my head.

"Piper, and no, she didn't even ask."

"Did you fuck her?" He grinned now, obviously feeling better enough to be crude.

"Really, dude?" I shook my head. "That's so classy."

"So that's affirmative. You fucked her." He started laughing then and checked his phone. "I'm wondering if I should cancel my trip to New York and fly to Orlando instead. What do you think?"

"I don't know. I don't think that's smart." I walked over to him and touched his shoulder. "Don't do anything out of the ordinary. There's no point."

"You sure you didn't tell that Piper anything?"

"She didn't ask me anything ..." I paused to think back to my conversation with Piper. "Well, I guess she kinda asked about my pre-fame days, but nothing much. Nothing detailed or searching ..." I stopped for a second and tried to think back to the beach. "Maybe she asked me about our friendship, though."

"What did she ask and what did she already know?"

"I think maybe she knew that we grew up together and we went to the same college." I sighed. "But maybe I told her that. I don't remember."

"But she didn't tell you she was a journalist, did she?"

"No." I grew angry again. "She didn't tell me that. She told me she wrote books, but she didn't want to tell me what she was working on now."

"Yeah, I wonder why." Jackson tapped his hands against the table. "I could ruin her career. It would take one call to Bill, and he'd make sure she never got hired again by any reputable media house."

"Who does she work for now?" I asked him, curious and slightly guilty. I didn't want to ruin Piper's career. I'd thought she and I had some sort of connection. Obviously, I'd been wrong.

"Don't know. Alexa was telling me something about how she was so proud of Piper for doing what she loved and mentioned how she'd written some articles that had made her a shit ton of money."

"Expose articles?"

"That's what I'm guessing." Jackson shook his head. "I should have known when she was faking not knowing you in the club that she was up to no good. Like who the hell doesn't know Oracle Lion?"

"A few people." I laughed, though I wasn't feeling happy. "She didn't seem to know my real name was Zach, though." I started pacing back and forth. "And she didn't mention the band."

"Yeah, because she's smart enough not to show her cards too soon," Jackson growled. "I need a beer." He walked towards the kitchen and I followed behind him. "Also, your mom called."

"Pass me a Bud," I said as he opened the fridge. "And maybe throw me a sandwich. I'm hungry."

"You didn't eat yet?"

"I was kinda occupied." I gave him a wink, and he laughed.

"And I'm the dirty dog?"

"You didn't hook up with Alexa?"

"Nah, she wanted to talk." He rolled his eyes. "Now I know why."

"They don't know anything, Jackson. There's no way they know anything. It'll be okay, man."

"Yeah, yeah." He took a deep breath. "I just thought that by now we'd be able to breathe easy, you know?" He shook his head. "But you can't trust any of these hoes."

"Yeah." I nodded as I popped the tab on the Bud can and started drinking. Piper's innocent smile and breathtaking face popped into my mind, and I tried to ignore the memory of her fingers digging into my shoulders as she climaxed. Her eyes had been so wide and full of emotion. She'd acted like I'd given her the best orgasm of my life. I snorted as I realized she'd been a better actress than I'd given her credit for. "She did say something weird to me, though."

"What?" He paused.

"She told me I'd given her inspiration for her next book." I clenched my fist. "And her friend, Alexa—well, her friend said she found out something about you."

"What?" Jackson looked nervous. "What did she find out?"

"That I don't know," I said in an agitated tone. "That I really don't know."

"We have to find out, Zach. This can't get out in the open." He stared at me for what felt like years, and I was taken back to our childhood and memories that I'd tried to forget. "It would ruin us both. It would ruin everything."

"I know." I squeezed his shoulder. "Leave it to me. I'll take care of it." I spoke in such a confident tone that almost I believed myself, but I didn't know what I was going to do. I'd have to think and plan. I knew that I had to do whatever it took. We hadn't come all this way for someone like Piper Meadows to make it all come crashing down. Not even with her cute impish smile and sexy long hair. She wasn't going to bewitch me again. I would make sure of that.

~

"HAVE A SAFE FLIGHT. I'll speak to you later."

I waved bye to Jackson as he got into the waiting limo then walked back to the dining room. I walked over to the table and picked up the newspaper so that I could read the full article and see what had gotten Jackson so nervous. Maybe he'd been working himself up for nothing. I could feel my heart racing as I stared at the photo and headline that took up the full front page of the *Orlando Sentinel* newspaper. The headline read, *The Case of Radley Markham—What Happened To the Billion Dollar Heir to the Markham Fortune?* And right below it was a photograph of Radley at Cocoa Beach with a surfboard.

I stared at the photo and grimaced as I looked in the background. Right behind Radley stood four other guys, all with surfboards, and two women in tiny bikinis. That photo had been taken the day before Radley had disappeared and that group was thought to have been the last people to have seen him alive.

I stared at the photo and bit down on my lower lip before scanning the article to see what was included, but it was the same information that had been given years and years ago. It just talked about how the elusive, handsome surfer Radley Markham, the sole heir to a pharmaceutical fortune, had disappeared. There was no mention of me or of Jackson, and why should there be? We'd never been mentioned in any of the previous articles.

The case had died down years ago, but if anyone looked carefully at the article now, any fans, the background of the photo might make them twice about the article. In that group of surfers stood younger versions of me and Jackson, and I knew that the press would go crazy if they ever realized we were part of the last group that had seen him alive. It might have been noted that we were in the same fraternity, but I don't think anyone had ever made the deep personal connection between us. And if they dug deeper, they'd find out even more about the beginnings of both of our careers.

I folded the newspaper and carried it to my study. I'd read it after I called my mom. As I settled into my plush leather chair behind my mahogany wood desk, I allowed myself to think of Piper again. Had she played me from the beginning? Had she slept with me just to get more access into my life? What was her next step? She hadn't even asked me for my number, but I had a feeling I'd be hearing from her soon enough. Women like her, users, always seemed to find a way to get back in touch.

"Hey, Mom, it's me. I heard you called." I sank back into my chair, knowing that the upcoming call was going to last for at least an hour. I pulled out a notepad and pen and started writing some notes. I needed to figure out what to do next because as I'd thought about it, I realized that Piper wasn't just planning on writing an article about mine and Jackson's history. She was planning on writing a whole book. And I wasn't about to let that happen.

CHAPTER 10

PIPER

"So what is it you found out?" I pulled the sheets up around me so that I didn't accidentally flash Alexa. "Actually, can we pause for fifteen minutes? I'd like to take a shower and put on some clothes."

"And maybe we can get some food, too." Alexa looked hopeful and I smiled as best as I could. "Hey, are you okay?" She lightly touched my shoulder. "I'm sorry that douchebag treated you like that. He thinks he's all that, but all he is is an asshole. Typical Hollyweird asshole."

"Yeah, you're right." I nodded and sighed. "My gut told me in the club he was full of shit and he was. I should have listened to my brain and not my body."

"You weren't to know, girl." Alexa stood up. "Neither one of us were to know. We haven't dealt with guys like these before."

"What, Hollywood stars?"

"Hollywood stars with a secret." She smiled at me mysteriously. "Shower and get dressed. I need to check something out online."

"Okay, Nancy Drew," I said as she walked towards the door. "I just hope that there are mimosas in my foreseeable future."

"Of course." She laughed. "How can we brunch in LA without them? Maybe we can even pay for them on dickwad's dime."

"Of course we will." I laughed. "He'll also be paying for the new LV bag I buy today. And this time, it's not going to be a fake."

"So what is it you found out?" I asked Alexa impatiently after we ordered our food. "You're killing me here. First, no mimosas and still no story." I gave her a look. "This had better be good."

"I'll tell you in a second," she said absentmindedly as she sipped on her corner. "Shit, I think I left my newspaper at Oracle's place." Alexa groaned as she put her coffee cup down. "Shit, shit, shit."

"What newspaper?" I asked her curiously and withheld a sigh. "What does that have to do with what you found out? And wait, you spent the night at Zach's?"

"Oops yeah, I forgot since we're his friends now, we can call him Zach."

"We're not his friends." I rolled my eyes and snorted. "Was it nice?"

"Was what nice?"

"His house?"

"It was large and looked modern, but I didn't love it." She made a face and then gasped. "Oh my God," she looked annoyed at herself. "I should have gone into the bathroom and looked through the cupboards.

"Oh, Alexa, no wonder Zach thinks we're shady." I laughed and then pressed some more. "Did you see any women's touches or ..." My voice trailed off. I knew I sounded pathetic.

"Or what?"

"Bras or stuff?"

"Oh Piper, are you jealous?" Her eyes widened as she giggled. "You don't have a thing for him, do you? Not after how he left? I guess he could just be one of those moody sorts of guys. Are you going to see him again?"

"Hell, no." I made a face. "He didn't get my number, and he didn't give me his, so no, I doubt it. And even if he did call, I wouldn't answer after how he treated me. Jerkface."

"True, he doesn't deserve you. But to answer your question, no I didn't see any evidence that a woman has ever been at his place." Alexa said with a small shrug. "To be honest, his place felt cold. Cold and gray and slightly ugly."

"But you still had fun, right? With Jackson?" I asked. "Before you left?"

"Honestly?" She looked at me with an unsure look on her face. "It was weird. He's not how I thought he would be."

"Oh?"

"Yeah, I don't know how to put it into words."

"Was he good in bed?"

"We didn't even have sex, girl." She shook her head. "I'm not sure if he didn't find me attractive or had had too much to drink or what. This morning, I thought we might, but he basically started shouting at me and kicked me out as soon as he woke up."

"Oh shit, what? What were you doing?" I wanted to ask her more about the night before but didn't want to pry. I could tell that there was something she wasn't telling me in her story but wasn't going to push it.

"Nothing. I was in bed reading the newspapers I got from the library."

"Oh, for your research?"

"Yeah." She nodded. "Maybe he thought I was too nerdy."

"Oh, sad." I walked over to give her a hug. "That sucks."

"I guess it's true what they say about famous guys. They look better than they are." She rolled her eyes. "Weirdo."

"That sucks."

"Yeah, who would have thought out of the two of us, you would be the one who got laid last night."

"Not me," I laughed. "Not me."

"It just sucks because there was a great article about the history of the KKK in Florida because they had a rally in downtown Orlando and one of the reporters did an extensive write-up."

"Aww man, that sucks. So you decided to make Florida one of the key states for your research?"

"Yeah." She nodded. "I think it's really interesting. You wouldn't think that Florida would have such a high concentration of white supremacists, but it does, and the history is really rich." She started playing with her hair, and I knew she was going into historian mode. "I want to link the ending of segregation to the rise of clan membership."

"The rise?" I blinked. "Oh wow, I wouldn't have thought that."

"Yeah." She sighed. "I mean I haven't got it all figured out yet, but it makes sense right because even after Brown vs. Board of Education, many cities in the South still didn't want to desegregate." She looked at me then. "I told you about that case in North Carolina, right?"

"Yeah." I looked down. My life choices were starting to feel insignificant. Alexa and I had both studied history in undergrad, but there she was working on her PhD and trying to figure out real solutions to societal issues, and here I was trying to write a sexy paranormal romance book. I'd tried my hand at historical romance and while it had been well regarded, I hadn't enjoyed writing it. And it also hadn't paid well.

I'd been lucky enough to get a side gig writing movie reviews for an online entertainment website and had gotten even luckier in having ten articles that had blown up and been syndicated around the world. Fortune had favored me, and the director of last year's Oscar winner who was working on the next superhero franchise was the father of one of Alexa's classmates, and she'd gotten me an exclusive. It had helped that she'd been sleeping with her classmate at the time and promised him we'd have a threesome if he'd get me the exclusive. I hadn't known about that offer until later when she'd dumped him for cheating on her with his latest step-sister. It had been a whole lot of drama at the time, but it had made me $50,000 richer and was the reason why I was now able to focus on writing my book about two star-crossed lovers who happened to be a vampire and a witch.

"But that's not all I wanted to tell you." She leaned forward with a conspiratorial grin and interrupted my thoughts.

"Oh?" I looked up at her and this time she had a wicked look on her face. "What is it, Alexa? Oh my God, please tell me."

"That newspaper, well, I got it for my research, but I ended up finding something else."

"What? What?" I was dying to know now.

"When Jackson started acting crazy and accusing me of being some sort of paparazzi, I saw his eyes darting to the front of the newspaper a lot."

"Okay, and?"

"There was a cover story on the front about some rich kid who disappeared."

"Aww, that's sad. How old were they?"

"Some guy, looked to be about eighteen or maybe twenty."

"Oh, so not a young kid. I thought you meant ..." I stopped talking when Alexa put her hand up in the air. "Sorry. Continue."

"So this rich kid was the heir to some fortune, and he disappeared."

"Yeah, okay."

"He was hanging out with friends the night before he died."

"He died?"

"Oh, I don't know. I assume he died, right? I mean it's been ages." She shrugged. "So I was checking out the photo and guess who I see in the background of the photo?"

"Who?" I asked. "Wait, not yourself?"

"Piper Meadows, sometimes you really are a blonde." She rolled her eyes at me. "How the hell am I going to see myself in the back of some photo of some guy that disappeared in Orlando when I've never even been to Florida?"

"I don't know, maybe you have a doppelganger?" I stopped then as I could see she was getting irritated. "Fine, sorry. Who did you see?"

"None other than Mr. Jackson Camden and Mr. Oracle Lion—sorry, Mr. Zach Houston."

"What?" My jaw dropped. "No way."

"Way. Younger versions, but it was them." She nodded to herself. "It was definitely them. That's why I took the photo this morning of the two of you. As evidence."

"Evidence of what?" I blinked at her, not understanding what she was saying.

"If you go missing, I can show the police you were with him."

"With Zach? Why would they care that I was ever with him and why would I go missing?" And then it hit me. "You think they had something to do with it?"

"Yes, Einstein." She grinned at my pout. "Sorry, I couldn't resist, but it makes sense, right? Why else did Jackson go so funny?" She looked away for a few seconds and I could see that she was thinking about something that she didn't want to talk about with me. "We need to find out what happened." She looked back at me suddenly. "Don't you want to know what happened?"

"Well, we don't even know if it was them or if they know what happened." I stopped talking as the waitress approached us with two plates. She placed my eggs benedict and home fries in front of me and the cheese and spinach omelette in front of Alexa. "Thank you," I said as she smiled at us and then as soon as she walked away I turned back to Alexa. "You're making a lot of assumptions."

"I'm a historian, that's my job." She grabbed her knife and fork and started eating. "I'm so hungry, it's not even funny."

"So we should make a list of all the things we think we know and go from there," I said as I picked up my cutlery. "Pass the salt and pepper, please." I took a bite and realized the hollandaise sauce was tasteless. "And how are we meant to find out anything more? Neither one of us has contact with either of them, and it's not like we hobnob with the rich and famous every day."

"We'll think of something," she said as she passed me the salt and pepper shakers. "Don't make that face at me, Piper. It'll be fun."

"I don't know about fun." I grabbed my orange juice, sans champagne, and took a sip. "What I do know is I want to see that newspaper article and photo for myself before we take any steps."

"I knew you'd be in." She grinned. "How exciting is this weekend turning out to be?"

"I had plenty of fun this morning, thanks."

I put my glass down and thought back to how Zach had pleasured me. He'd taken control, and I'd seen a sexy, dominant side to him that I wouldn't have guessed existed. When he'd told me to say his name, he'd been so insistent, so teasing. It had made me want him even more. The look in his eyes had been tantalizing, and I knew in my heart of hearts that he had even more secrets hidden inside that I couldn't even guess at. He could be cocky, self-deprecating, bossy, even humorous at times, but behind it all, there was a cloud of something else. Something impenetrable. Zach Houston definitely had a secret hidden past; something that he was holding inside.

Normally, I would have let it go. It wasn't my business after all. Yes, the sex had been great, and I'd never expected to see him again after our one-night stand, but after he'd left that money, no, *thrown* that money on the bed and given me that arrogant look of disdain, I wasn't just going to let it go.

CHAPTER 11

Oracle

"Zach, I've been thinking and wondering ..." My mother's voice trailed off, and I could feel myself tensing at what was going to come next. Nothing ever good came from my mom thinking.

"Yes?" I said finally when she didn't continue. I hated it when she did this. She wanted me to coax her thoughts out of her as if I were dying to hear her story.

When I was a young child, it had been exciting, wondering what my mother was going to tell me. The long, painstaking details of her life had made me feel like she was confiding in me, like we were bonding, until I reached my teenage years and realized that my mom was an attention-seeking drama queen who thrived off of being admired and heard. It didn't help that now most of her friends had disappeared and we had little to no family other than each other. I had become my mom's everything, and she didn't know how to let go of the past or me.

"Why do you have an attitude, Zach? Is that any way to talk to your mother?" Her voice rose, and I knew that if I didn't soothe her right away, she'd have some sort of emotional breakdown.

"I don't have an attitude, Mom, I just don't have time for a long story right now. I'm working on something new and, well, it's time-sensitive." I tried to be as polite as possible without completely lying.

"You always make time for work and other people," she said and I took a deep breath. If she started to complain about how little time I had for her, I was going to shit a brick. "I was thinking about my parents and how their story is so unique."

"Okay?" I asked her wondering where this was going. My mom had been raised by her mom and stepfather who had immigrated to the States from England. My grandfather, her birth father, had died in World War II in the trenches in France, and my grandmother would sometimes have dreams of him coming to her. He had been the love of her life and everyone knew it; even her new husband, who had, quite rightly, in my opinion, ended up leaving her when my mom was five. Nana had worked as a housekeeper for a rich family in South Carolina who had liked the fact that she had an English accent, and my mom had grown up with the kids in the family, taking on all their heirs and graces as if her ancestors had been owners of a vast plantation as well.

"Have you thought about making a movie about them?" she said, her voice bright. "Didn't that Steven Spielberg make that one war movie that did really well?"

"*Saving Private Ryan?*" I asked cautiously.

"Hmm no, that doesn't sound right. The one in the war with the nurse. And she fell in love with the soldier."

"*The English Patient?*"

"No, no, that's not it. Was it called *The Hangover?*" Her voice sounded genuine, and I withheld a laugh.

"No, Mom, I don't think you're thinking about *The Hangover*, but anyways, what about it?"

"I think you could win an Oscar if you made a movie about your grandparents and their epic love story. It would be a lot to know you have a personal connection to the story."

"Mom, I don't even know their story, not really." I took a deep breath. "So it would be hard to make a movie about it."

"Well, I can tell you everything and you can write it down and make it. Doug, be quiet." She shushed her yappy dog who was barking up a storm in the background.

"Mom, you know I'm not a writer."

"You wrote those songs when you were in that band with Jackson and Radley. What was it called again?"

"Three Donkeys," I said trying not to grimace. How often was Radley going to come up today?

"Oh yeah, the three horses. Well, you wrote those songs. You can write a book about your grandparents. It's the least you can do, Zach."

"Mom," I sighed, "that doesn't make me a writer."

"Well, don't you know plenty of writers?" She continued pushing it. "You're telling me the number one actor in all of Hollywood doesn't know any writers? And don't forget where you came from, young man. If it wasn't for Nana moving and working as a slave to support us, you wouldn't be where you are today."

"Mom, Nana didn't work as a slave. You can't make those comments."

"Well, she worked as a housekeeper and nanny in the South, it's almost the same thing."

"Mom, you and Nana had your own wing in the house. The Cornelius family also sent you to private school, and Mr.

Cornelius gave Nanna two hundred thousand dollars when she retired. It's not quite the same."

"Well, you know what I'm saying. I'm not saying she was a *slave* slave, though she did also come over to this country on a boat."

"Mom. It's not the same thing. She took a boat to Ellis Island of her own free will." I closed my eyes for a few seconds and took a deep breath.

"You are such a snowflake, Zach. My friend Iris was telling me all about you liberal Hollywood actors and your agenda. Well, you know I never—"

"Mom, I'm not going to listen to this right now, okay. I don't know who your friend Iris is, but if she's the one feeding you this crap, you need to drop her because she's not a good friend."

"Well, now Zach, there's no need to go getting into a mood. I'm just telling you what she told me. Everyone's so sensitive these days. You can't say anything."

"Mom, you're an attractive white woman with blonde hair and blue eyes, you live in a million-dollar house, you have a Mercedes, you and Nana were never slaves, and it's disrespectful to say you were."

"I never said *I* was a slave, Zach. I just said—"

"MOM! Stop, please." I couldn't deal with her nonsense today. Not after the day I'd already had. I had bigger things to worry and think about.

"Are you going to make Nanna's movie? I think she'd love to know her dear grandson made a movie about her love story."

"Let me think about it, okay? Look, Mom, I have to go. I'll call you later. Maybe next week."

"Fine. I'm here and ready to tell you the story when you make time." She paused and then she said. "I saw the Orlando

Sentinel today. Top story was about Radley. Looks like there might be some new information in the case."

"Oh?" I asked, my heart going still. What information?

"Yes, my friend Iris, well, her grandson is a deputy sheriff, and he works for the OPD. Transferred up from West Palm Beach a couple of years after she downsized. He still comes to see her every month, as well. He's a good boy."

"That's nice, Mom."

"She has a granddaughter as well, Zoe is her name. A sweet thing she is, but they're Jewish, and I know Iris has her heart set on a Jewish husband for Zoe, though I suppose she wouldn't say no to a famous Hollywood star as a grandson-in-law, Jewish or not."

"Mom, I told you a long time ago that we're not discussing my love life."

"Well, you don't want to be single forever. I saw that you and that Cassie Cash broke up. What you need is a real woman, a nice young lady, Zach. Not one of those stick-thin models or actresses. You know how they stay so thin? It's cocaine. Iris told me."

"Well, Iris seems to know a lot, doesn't she?" I didn't want to confirm anything, but that was a piece of information that Iris had gotten correct. "And I do date plenty of real women who aren't in the business, Mom." An image of Piper flashed through my mind, but I dismissed it as easily as it had come. I wasn't dating her, and she was as far from a real woman as you could find. She was a two-faced snake.

"Good good, so I'll hear from you about the movie? You don't even have to come to Florida. I'll fly to LA." She started singing under her breath. "I have to go now, my love. I need to go to the mall and look for some clothes. See you soon. Stay good, Zachy. Love you."

And with that, she was gone.

I put the phone down on my desk and stood up. I walked towards the doorway and down the long corridor to the kitchen. The house was too big for one person, and it was so grey. The only part of the house I loved was the large pool outside the living room. I walked towards the living room and opened the sliding door and made my way over to the pool. I slowly took off my shirt and pants and left them on the ground. I pulled off my briefs, threw them towards my pants and then dove into the deep end.

I loved swimming naked. I loved the water. I held my breath and swam the entire length of the pool, even though the pool was Olympic-sized. I could feel myself running low on oxygen in my lungs, but I wasn't going to surface until I hit the wall. I couldn't. I had to reach the end. My hand tapped the wall and I surfaced gasping for air, the water rushing down my face. I ran my hands through my hair and leaned back against the side of the pool. The blue of the water shimmered in the sunlight and I stared at it for a few seconds. The sky blue color of the water was the exact same shade as Radley's eyes. Radley Markham. Radley Markham. Radley Markham. My first friend.

I'd actually met him before I met Jackson. His mother had been a distant cousin of the Kennedys, and my mother had made sure to become Mrs. Radley's friend in the mommy group she'd joined as soon as she'd found out that fact. Mrs. Markham had been a nice lady, young, sweet, impressionable. Her much older husband had been the opposite, though. He'd been a nasty piece of work. A controlling man. Abusive. A cheat. Mrs. Markham had taken her own life when Radley was just ten. I felt like it had affected me more than Radley. And maybe even more than my mom.

I slapped the water in frustration as I thought of my mom. I loved her, I really did. I loved her because she was my mom and she was a good person underneath it all, but boy she made it hard. On the surface, she was a busybody, a snob, and maybe to some a racist, but I knew that she held a hurt she'd never gotten over. She had fallen in love when she was sixteen with an African American boy by the name of Marcus Martin. She'd talked about him so much that I knew his name better than my own. He'd been a scholarship student in her class, and he had loved her as well. They'd even gone on a couple of dates. And then my Nana had found out. And God bless my Nana, but she had been a racist and she had banned my mom from dating him. My mom, ever the stubborn woman that she was, said no and kept on dating him. And then something had happened. I didn't know what exactly, but they'd broken up.

Two years after that she met and married my dad, good old Johnson Houston, a banker who had been twenty years older than her and a handsome stud. Two years later she still hadn't gotten pregnant and was wondering what was going on. She was a bit wishy-washy about what happened next in the marriage, but all of a sudden, when she was thirty-nine years old, she'd gotten pregnant with me. And my dad had died when I was three, leaving her to raise me alone. I had very few memories of my dad asides from his kind laugh and him singing "Yankee Doodle Dandy" to me every night.

When Radley's mother had died, I'd tried to talk to him and offer some support. I'd told him that it got better, that even though I missed my dad every day, I knew he was in a better place. Radley had just stared at me with blank, unfeeling eyes. It had been the strangest thing, and at the time, I was uncomfortable and worried about my friend. It took a few years before my feelings towards him started changing and the worry I felt towards him had changed to something more akin to hatred. Radley Markham had been handed the world on a plate and he didn't even appreciate it.

And the only one that knew was Jackson. Jackson Camden, the one person in the world I trusted my life with. The one person who had been genuine with me from the beginning. We'd been together on the way up, and we'd be together on the way down. I'd cross heaven and hell for him.

And it looked like I might be about to.

CHAPTER 12

PIPER

"I'LL HAVE A GREEN TEA, PLEASE." I smiled at the barista at the new Starbucks in Montclair Village and kept my eyes averted from the iced lemon loaf slices.

"What size?"

"Grande, please." I debated getting a toasted bagel. "Actually, I'm sorry to do this, but can I get a grande mocha frappuccino and a toasted plain bagel with butter?"

"Any cream cheese?" the barista asked me, and I shook my head.

"No, thanks. I'm trying to be healthy," I said with a small laugh. "So hold the whipped cream as well, please."

"No whipped cream?"

I bit down on my lower lip and sighed. The whipped cream with a squirt of chocolate syrup made the drink. "Go on, then. I can start my diet over tomorrow," I said with a wide grin, but she didn't grin back.

"Name?"

"Piper." I handed her over a twenty-dollar bill. She handed me back my change without saying another word. I debated cracking a joke about her having a bad day but decided to keep my mouth shut.

I looked around and hurried over to an open table that had just opened up next to the window. The view wasn't the most picturesque, but I'd take looking at the stores across the street overlooking at the baristas working.

I had a lot to get done today. I wanted to outline my book and I knew that Alexa wanted to meet up with me later to discuss what our next steps should be with the Jackson and Zach investigation. It made me feel a bit like Harriet the Spy or Nancy Drew and all sorts of cool until I actually started thinking about what we were doing. These were rich powerful men, and we were insignificant nobodies whose only experience with detective work was playing the Sherlock Holmes Consulting Detective Agency board game.

I pulled out my laptop and my notebook, glancing towards the counter to make sure they hadn't already made my drink and called out my name. I picked up my phone and scrolled to see if I had any text messages and tried to ignore the wash of disappointment that flooded through me when I saw that the only message I had was from my cousin. Nothing from Zach.

Which wasn't surprising because he didn't have my number. And he was an asshole, but still. I'd hoped that maybe he'd have an explanation for everything and that he would text or call me to apologize for dumping that money on the bed. He'd been so rude, and I found it hard to reconcile the man who had danced with me on the beach and kissed me so sweetly with the man that had thrown the money on the bed with the coldest expression I'd ever seen in my life.

"Piper, one grande mocha frappuccino ready," a man called out.

I jumped up and headed over to collect my drink, looking back at my table quickly to make sure that no thieves were going to steal my laptop as I got my drink. I always worried when I went to coffee shops and the beach. What were you meant to do with your stuff when you got up? I mean, there's a system of trust, but really, who knows who will break that trust?

I grabbed my drink and headed back to my table. I grabbed my pen and started doodling on the pad. This was my first time writing paranormal romance, and I knew that I was going to make it steamy. I was going to model the vampire on Zach—well, my fantasy of Zach, not the real Zach. He was brooding and handsome and the things he had done in bed were definitely going to be featured in the sex scenes I wrote.

I found myself doodling and writing Zach's name over and over on my pad, so I opened my laptop and decided to do some research instead. I typed "Oracle Lion" into the Google search bar and waited to see what popped up on the screen.

My phone beeped and I grabbed it to see a text from Alexa.

"Got another copy of the paper. Where are you?"

"At Starbucks in the village. Don't you have a meeting with your advisor now?"

"It was canceled. Coming now."

"I can come to Berkeley if you want?"

"Nah, it's cool. We can grab some groceries at Lucky's afterwards."

"Yeah, sounds good."

"See you in a few."

I put my phone down and leaned back in my chair.

"Piper, one toasted plain bagel with butter."

I jumped up to grab my bagel and walked slowly back to

my chair. Something that Alexa had said had been bothering me all weekend, and I was having trouble identifying exactly what it was. I sipped on my drink as I thought back to our trip to Los Angeles. Alexa had organized the trip because she thought we'd needed a getaway from our mundane lives in Oakland. I had been quite happy to go along with her and the drive to LA had been fun.

I froze as I realized what was bothering me. Alexa had wanted us to go on a girls' trip, but she'd immediately gone onto Tinder and gone on a date. Not only that, she'd told me to meet her at the club by myself and then had arrived late. As soon as she'd arrived she'd gone off with Jackson. It just didn't make sense to me. Why had Alexa arranged a girls' trip just to search for a man?

I sighed as I realized I was going to have to talk to her about her behavior. It was not acceptable to me that she had put dating and hooking up with a rando before me. That's not what friends did.

"Wow," I mumbled under my breath as the first article popped up on the screen. *Hollywood Star Oracle Lion Thought To Be Dating Princess Maria Villanova of Spain* screamed the headline. I clicked on the article and saw a photo of Zach and a beautiful woman with long straight black hair, big blue eyes, and a wide smile. She looked like a young Elizabeth Taylor, and my heart sunk. No wonder Zach hadn't asked for my number. Why would he when he had his choice of all the women in the world?

I quickly skimmed the article and then looked down to read the comments, which were often my favorite part of the articles I read. Most of the comments were about the fact that he went from woman to woman, with one man giving him a virtual high-five for being the playboy of the century. I rolled my eyes at that one, but then my heart started racing as I read the next comment from Spacecoast69, "How many women are you going to steal from better men? Or should I keep my mouth shut? I don't want to go missing."

I reread the comment about fifty times and my body went hot. "Holy shit," I blurted out loudly. The older man sitting to the right of me gave me a disapproving look, and I offered him an apologetic smile. "Sorry," I said and grabbed my phone to text Alexa.

"OH MY GOSH, you will not believe what I just found. Where are you?"

"What did you find? I'll be there in about twenty minutes."

"I'll show you when you get here, but I think we have a break in the case."

"Omg, I need to see. Does that give me permission to speed?"

"No. Drive safely. See you soon."

I put the phone back down on the table and tried to click on Spacecoast69's name to see if I can find out any other information on him or her, but there was no clickable link on the name. I copied the name and pasted it in a Google search to see if it brought up any other posts or a way for me to identify who this person was. Ten results popped up on the screen and I was about to click on the first link when my phone rang. I grabbed it and answered it without looking at the screen, my mind still preoccupied on the comment I'd just read.

A deep husky voice sounded in my ear. "Piper Meadows, is that you?" I knew who it was immediately.

"Zach?"

"The only and only."

I wanted to slap myself at the small leap of happiness that filled me. "What do you want?" I snapped. Who did he think he was calling me so casually after what he'd done?

"Wanted to know if you missed me yet?"

"Are you fucking joking?"

The man next to me gave me a disgusted look and stood

up, grabbing his newspaper and walking away. Talk about a drama queen.

"Language, Piper, language."

"What do you want, John?"

"John?" There was confusion in his voice. "Who the hell is John?"

"Aren't you John? If I'm a prostitute wouldn't you be John?" My voice held an edge to it that I hadn't heard before in my life. Frankly, I impressed myself with the attitude I was giving him. I was cool, calm and collected, but let him know I was over him.

"Oh ..." He chuckled. "That was a joke."

"No, it wasn't."

"I want to see you again."

I didn't answer him because my heart had suddenly started racing and I wanted to scream out, *When?* My brain was on a different level though and was screaming, *Hell no!*

"Piper?"

"That's my name."

"Can I see you again?"

"Why? So you can fuck me and leave twenty grand?" I whispered into the phone this time. I didn't need to get kicked out of Starbucks.

"Twenty grand, eh? Your rate went up."

"You're such an asshole, you know that right?" I was about to hang up when he spoke again.

"You're right, and I want to make it up to you. I have a proposition for you."

"What proposition?"

"It's nothing like that." His voice was serious all of a sudden. "It's related to your writing." He stressed the last word in a weird way and I frowned. Had I mentioned my paranormal story to him in my sleep or something?

"What about it?"

"I want you to write a screenplay for me."

"A screenplay?"

"Yes, for a movie."

"A movie? What movie?"

"I'll tell you more if you meet up with me. You know you want to."

"I'm not meeting up with you, Oracle Lion," I said in my coldest voice. Who the hell did he think he was?

"So I'm back to being Oracle now?"

"Yes, Oracle. Why don't you go and meet up with Princess Maria and don't bother calling me again."

I hung up before I changed my mind and told him to come over to dinner or something. As much as I hated how he'd treated me, I was still intrigued by him. And he had been dynamite in bed, so it wasn't like I didn't want to sleep with him again. Oh boy, my body would love to sleep with him again. But then there was also the issue of him possibly being involved with Radley Markham's disappearance. And I didn't know what the comment was about, but had he also stolen some women as well? Who was the real Zach Houston and exactly what was he capable of?

I didn't know, and I wasn't sure that I wanted to find out.

CHAPTER 13

Zach

"She hung up on me." I looked at the phone in my hand in shock. "She bloody hung up on me."

I lay back on my plush white couch and stared at the painting of a surfer in Hawaii that hung over my fireplace. I loved the painting and it always calmed me down. I debated phoning Piper back, but I wasn't sure if she would even answer the phone.

So that hadn't gone according to plan. I jumped up off of the couch and walked the short distance to the kitchen, looking down at the colorful rug I'd had shipped back from a bazaar while I'd been in Marrakech, Morocco. It was made of bright red and blue wool, and its vibrant colors were a vast change from my other house. That was a house, This was my home.

I opened the fridge and pulled out the bottle of orange juice and grabbed a glass. "Piper Meadows hung up on me." I smiled to myself as I took a sip of the freshly squeezed juice. That hadn't happened to me in years. In fact, I think the last time a woman had hung up on me had been in college. The smile left my face when I remembered who it was that had hung up on me.

"I hate you, Zach," she'd said.

"Can we meet up and talk?" I'd said. "I'd like you to—"

"I never want to see you again."

"Just one more time, just let me explain," I'd pleaded and then she'd hung up.

I'd been shocked and worried. I'd known that I'd had to fix that situation, not just for me but for Jackson as well. Of course, nothing had gone according to plan.

I grabbed my phone and called Jackson. He was the only person I could speak to right now.

"Yo, Yo, what's up Houston?"

"You're in a good mood."

"I just booked Madison Square Garden, dude. And my world tour has been green-lit. Thirty-two countries in six months. It's going to be epic."

"Wow, that's awesome."

"You should have stayed in the band." Jackson laughed, but I didn't join in his mirth.

"There was no band once Radley left, dude."

"He was a muthafucka, wasn't he?" Jackson seemed to sober up at my words. "So did you talk to Piper? When's she going down to LA again?" He paused. "And do you think Alexa will visit her?"

"She's not coming. She hung up on me. She didn't even listen to my offer."

· "What?" He sounded panicked. "What do you mean? You told her about writing the movie, right? That's an amazing opportunity. Is she stupid?"

"Well, she's not that stupid if she's writing a book about us, is she?"

"So that's confirmed?" Jackson's voice was low now. "You need to figure out exactly what they know. We need to get on top of this, Zach."

"What am I supposed to do?"

"Beg her to help?"

"I don't beg."

"Have your mom contact her. Tell her that Piper's the best writer in the business and that she needs to convince her to write this script. Tell her that you'll only make the movie if she can get Piper to sign on." He chuckled then. "Your mom doesn't take no for an answer, ever. She'll get Piper to sign up."

"But we don't actually want my mom involved, remember? What if Piper starts asking her questions?"

"Your mom doesn't know what happened, does she?"

"No, of course she doesn't know." I sighed. "You know that. But she does know about our friendship with Radley, and she knows a lot of other stuff that would be useful to Piper if she's writing a book. Useful to her and detrimental to—"

"Us," he cut me off. "I know, but we need to stay on top of this. We need to figure out what's going on."

"We don't even know if she's writing a book, Jackson. Come on, now. I called her. She's not interested. In fact, it makes me think she's not writing a book. If she was, wouldn't she have jumped for an excuse to see me again?"

"Not after you threw that money on her like some whore," Jackson grunted. "Obviously, she has some self-respect."

"She's not a whore." I clenched my fist. "I was just angry and confused. I didn't want to hurt her."

"She's trying to hurt us."

"No, we don't actually know that." I shook my head and I walked over to the window over the kitchen sink and looked out at the ocean in the distance. I could see the waves crashing into each other and I remembered that night on the beach with Piper. She'd been so carefree and relaxed. She hadn't had an agenda that night. I truly believed that. I didn't think she'd slept with me to get any information, and the fact that she'd hung up on me led me to believe that she wouldn't do any and everything for a story.

"We don't know that, but we do know that she and her friend have been very cagey."

"Her friend? You mean, Alexa? The woman you hooked up with?"

"I hook up with a lot of women. I don't always remember their names."

"But you just mentioned her name, not less than five minutes ago."

"I'm a rockstar. I've done a lot of drugs." He tried to laugh, but the sound was weak.

"What's going on here, Jackson?" I heard the clock in my living room chime and glanced at my watch. "Shit, I got to get going. I've got a meeting in Burbank later today."

"Oh, with who?"

"Tarantino."

"You're fucking kidding me, Tarantino?"

"Yeah." I grinned at his tone. "He wants me for a movie."

"Who else?"

"Charlize. Leo. Maybe Samuel, too."

"What about Brad?"

"I think he's committed for the next two years."

"Of course." Jackson laughed. "Well, if they need anyone for the score, you know who would kill it."

"Yeah, let me get the role first. We're just talking. My

agent thought it would be good as QT won't let anyone see the script until they've signed an NDA, and well, you know how it goes."

"Yeah, yeah, too cool, man. You don't sound excited."

"You know I want to make my own movie."

"I know. Like you made those band videos for us back in high school. They were epic."

"They were childish."

"Dude, they were epic. I still have them in my parents' garage. We should watch them next time we're home."

"Yeah, yeah, of course, man." We both knew that that was never going to happen. Neither one of us went back to Florida much, and even if we were both there, we wouldn't want to watch videos of us goofing around with Radley. Too many memories. Too many decisions that could have been made differently.

"So what are we going to do?" Jackson whispered. "If Piper is writing a book and it's about us, it will ruin everything, Zach. You won't be making any more movies. I won't be touring, and who knows what else will happen. Those girls are smart, dude. They found us. I didn't even know about that club until I got that email from Ringo, and I told you Ringo told me he never sent it to me, right? We only went there because of him. It seems mighty convenient to me that I got some mystery email about some club and they both show up and have their wicked way with us."

"Let me think about it," I said quickly, feeling stressed again. "I'll call you back later."

"Okay."

I hung up and walked back to my office. It hadn't been hard getting Piper's phone number. I'd typed in her name in Google and then put history and Oakland and pressed search. The fifth entry had listed fourteen different phone numbers for her and she'd answered on the third call I'd made. I sat back down in my chair and opened my laptop back up. This time I needed to find out some real information on Piper, information that I was getting for myself and not just from Jackson's imagination.

First thing I wanted to figure out was what books she'd written already. Maybe that would give me some insight into the way her mind worked. She'd said she was a historian, and now I was kicking myself for not asking her what area of history. For all I knew, she had ten books about cold cases and a podcast with a million listeners.

And then I started laughing when I saw the covers of the two books that Piper had written popping up on Amazon. *The Highlander's Naughty Bride (A Steamy Scottish Romance Novel)* was the title of the first book and the cover featured a shirtless man with long black hair and bulging muscles holding a petite redhead with a shy smile to his chest. The background featured what I assumed was a castle set in the highlands of Scotland. I noticed that the book was available in both paperback and a digital format.

"Knew I should have gotten that Kindle," I mumbled to myself as I bought the book and downloaded the Kindle app on my phone. It took about a minute to download and then the book cover popped up on the screen. I clicked on the cover. I was excited to read Piper's book even I knew that there wasn't going to be some big expose on Scottish clansmen in the pages. Still, I was curious to read words that had flowed from her brain. I decided that I wanted to read the book in a more comfortable space and so got up to head to the bedroom to relax.

"Shit, shit, shit." I stopped halfway down the corridor. I had almost forgotten that I had my meeting. I couldn't afford to miss the meeting. Getting this role would put me right at the top of the Hollywood A-list. Once I was there, I could make any movie that I wanted to. Absolutely any movie at all.

～

"Oh, my lord, please wake up. It's morning and your duties await."

"Amelia, how many times do I have to tell you to not enter my bedroom in the morning." Lord Mcintosh scowled at the fair maiden, her cheeks flush and pink.

"But, my lord, the sun is already high in the sky and the birds are singing."

"Birds do not sing, Amelia." Lord Mcintosh arose from the bed with no shirt on and Amelia Abernathy knew that she should look away, but she couldn't stop herself from peering at his chest under lowered eyes. Callum Mcintosh glanced at his ward and hid a dark smile as he strode towards her. With her long red hair and big blue eyes, she was a picture to behold, but she was far too untoward and capricious for a lady. Her father, clan leader John Campbell had left Amelia with Callum and his Aunt Suzie while he had gone to Parliament, and it seemed to Callum that John was hoping he would take her as a wife. But Callum Mcintosh didn't have any plans on making an innocent virgin his wife. He had a proclivity for the late night clubs of London, and Amelia was not the sort of woman he could see enjoy his lifestyle."

I SMILED to myself as I finished reading the last paragraph of chapter one and grabbed my phone. This was what I needed after my meeting from earlier in the day. It had been so long and intense and the whole time I'd been there I'd been thinking about Piper. Before I could stop myself, I rang Piper's number again and waited to see if she would answer. Tapping my fingers against my bed sheet, I only realized I was holding my breath when she answered the phone.

"Hello?" She sounded angry.

"It's Zach."

"I know."

"What proclivities did Callum have in that he didn't think Amelia could keep up with?"

"Huh?"

"Did the Scottish lord have a thing for sex clubs?" I grinned into the phone as I heard her breathing. "Or is that rather your thing?" I started laughing at her sharp intake of breath. "You can tell me, Piper, I won't tell anyone. Promise."

"Wh-what are you talking about?" She tripped over her words, and I laughed even harder.

"*The Highlander's Naughty Bride*," I said in a serious voice. "Written by Piper Meadows, sex club partaker."

"I don't go to sex clubs!" she protested.

"Really? It was only the one time, then?"

"What was only one time?" She paused. "Oh." She said finally adding two and two together. "Why are you calling me?"

So she wasn't in the mood for playful banter, then? Not that I was surprised. In fact, I would have been shocked if she had flirted back with me in any way. Shocked and on high alert. Because the only way Piper Meadows would sound happy to hear from me would be if she was really writing a book about me and wanted an inside view of my life.

"I wanted to apologize."

"Oh?"

I knew I had her attention then. I had surprised myself as much as I had surprised her. I never apologized. I didn't even recognize who I was right now; it was like some part of me had forgotten to be the cold and indifferent person that I normally was.

"What are you apologizing for?" she prompted me when I didn't continue talking.

128

I grinned into the phone, feeling the first genuine smile on my face in days. I wanted—no, *needed* to see her.

"Can I tell you in person?"

"In person?" I could hear the frown in her voice. "I don't live in LA, remember? And you also never told me how you got my phone number."

"The internet is a wonderful invention, Piper Meadows. You can learn many interesting facts about people there." I cleared my throat as I thought quickly. "But I was thinking we could meet up in San Francisco. You're in Oakland, right? I'm actually heading up there tomorrow for a meeting with some software engineers about a tech startup I'm investing some funds in. Maybe we could meet later in the day if you're free?"

"You're going to be in San Francisco?"

"Yes." I was lying through my teeth. I had no plans to be up in the Bay Area, but that was the good thing about being rich and famous. You could make almost anything happen at the drop of a hat. "I'll text you tomorrow afternoon with a time and place to meet. Maybe we can grab dinner?"

"I don't know."

The phone went silent for a while and I decided to keep my mouth shut. I knew if I pushed her too hard, she would just say no, and I couldn't have her saying no. I needed to talk to her, needed to see her. And if I was being honest with myself, I needed to touch her as well. She had been in my head since I'd met her, and it wasn't just because I wanted to know if she was planning on writing a tell-all on me and Jackson. There was just no way she could know much of anything, I thought to myself, but that was a lie. There were several loose ends that Jackson and I hadn't been able to take care of, and any of those loose ends could lead back to us in a really bad way.

"I don't know if it's a good idea, Zach. I just have no

interest in seeing you again, to be honest. We had our fun and well, one night was enough for me. I'm afraid the hype was bigger than the man."

Then she hung up on me again.

This time my jaw dropped so wide open that ten flies and a couple of spiders could have made my mouth their abode and there still would have been space for more visitors. I dropped the phone on my sheets and got up. I needed to go for a swim, but this time it was going to be in the ocean. The ocean was like my safe space. It had been since I was a little kid, though I had to admit I was more at home in the warmer waters of the Atlantic. My favorite beach was in Tampa Bay in a place called Treasure Island, and it had the same turquoise blue waters as the Carribean.

When we were in college, Radley, Jackson, and I would take weekend trips just to go to the beach. All three of us had an affinity for the water. Our surfboards were our second home, and in college, we'd all wanted to become pro surfers. Radley had been the best of all of us though. He had a natural talent of riding the waves that had surpassed both Jackson's and my abilities, which is what made it all so ironic.

I sighed deeply as memories of the past came back. It had all happened so quickly. He'd known too much. We'd all been too drunk. We hadn't been thinking. I blocked the memory out and grabbed my phone again. I wasn't going to sleep well until I knew what was going on. I couldn't have this hanging over my head.

"Piper, don't hang up," I said before she could speak as she answered the phone. "I know what I did was rude, and I want a chance to explain. Five minutes is all I ask. I'll even come over to Oakland. How does that sound? You can pick the place."

Silence filled the line, but I knew she was listening because I could hear her breathing. "Five minutes. Please?"

"Fine," she said. "I'll text you a place tomorrow." And with that, she hung up. I didn't care though. I fist-pumped the air and then called Boris, a private pilot to see if he had his Cessna available for the next two days. Now I had to make a trip up to San Francisco, and I was hoping that I was going to be able to spend the night.

CHAPTER 14

PIPER

"WAS THAT HIM AGAIN?" Alexa hovered over me excitedly as I put the phone down next to me. "Wow, he's really into you."

"I don't want to see him." I bit down on my lower lip, my heart racing. I couldn't believe that Zach had called me again and had apologized. I still didn't understand why he'd been so rude, and I didn't really want to see him again, even though the sex had been amazing.

"You can ask him some questions." Alexa sat next to me on the couch and I could see her thinking how to phrase her next sentence without getting me mad. "We weren't able to find anything about him and Radley or Jackson. And we have no links as to what Spacecoast69 was trying to say. This way, we can find out if he has information."

"Oh *we* can, can we?"

"Piper, I know he's an asshole and perhaps a murderer or a kidnapper or a sex trafficker, but—"

"But?" I laughed disbelievingly at her words. "Aren't any of those things scary enough? You still want me to meet up with him?"

"We can find out the answers." She stared into my eyes. "This is important."

"I don't need any answers. I don't even know who Radley is. I never heard of him before the other day. And if this is the only way I will get to learn more about him, then I don't want to know."

"You said you wanted to get to the bottom of this." Alexa made a face. "Come on, Piper."

"Why do you care so much?" I looked at my best friend and she looked away nervously. "What's going on here, Alexa. What aren't you telling me?"

"Nothing." She jumped up off the couch. "I'm going to get a shower."

"Alexa!"

She stopped to look back at me, emotion written all over her face. Why was this affecting her so much?

"You know you can trust me with anything, right? I won't judge you and I won't ever be mad at anything."

Her eyes crinkled and she smiled at me. "I know, girl. I know." She wavered for a second and then sighed. "Look, there is more. I can't tell you now, but I will when I can. I promise."

"I'm meeting him tomorrow. For a drink." I bit down on my lower lip. "I didn't say yes for the story, though. I want to see him. I want to know why—well, you know."

"Are you falling for him, Piper?" Alexa's expression changed to one of worry. "I know you fall fast, but you know you don't even know him, right? He's an actor. Just because we've seen his movies doesn't mean we know him."

"I know I don't know him." I wrinkled my nose and

sighed. "But we had a moment. I really felt like we had a moment. I guess I was just imagining it."

"Maybe not. He does want to see you again. Maybe there's something there." She came back towards me. "Don't fall for him, Piper. We can scratch everything if you think you're going to fall for him. This whole thing isn't worth breaking your heart."

"We only had sex. It was a one-night stand. We didn't promise undying love to each other. I never thought I'd see him again."

"I know." She nodded and gave me a quick hug. "Just be careful. And meet him in a public place."

"What exactly do you want me to find out?" I asked her softly, thinking back to our meeting in Starbucks earlier. She'd been so eager to show me the article and the photo of a young Zach and Jackson. I was surprised that no one had recognized them in the photo, but it seemed like the story had never been syndicated and gone national. If Alexa hadn't gotten the *Orlando Sentinel* for her research, we never would known, either.

But really, what did we know? We knew that the two men had been friends with a missing man. We knew that someone had left a weird comment under an article about Zach dating someone. And that someone had inferred that Zach had been responsible for someone going missing, which may or may not have had something to do with Radley Markham's disappearance. Neither Alexa or I had been able to find out much information about Radley Markham, either. It was all quite suspicious, but it wasn't really my business.

And, well, I didn't think that Zach could be involved in something nefarious. Granted, I didn't know him well, but I felt like I'd connected with him. Under other circumstances, I could have seen myself dating him. I didn't understand why he wanted to meet up with me and talk so badly, though.

What did he care if I thought he was an asshole? He *had* been an asshole. What sort of gentleman threw money at a woman?

I SAT at the back of Kells, an Irish pub in the financial district of San Francisco, and sipped on a glass of water while watching a baseball game on the screen opposite from me. I tried breathing deeply to control my nerves and deliberately stopped myself from looking towards the entrance. Zach was five minutes late and my anxiety was at an all-time high. Was he going to stand me up? After practically begging me to meet him and then texting back and forth with me all day, was he going to just stand me up? For some reason, this made me inexplicably upset. I honestly felt like I was on the verge of tears. I took another sip of water. I'd give him ten more minutes and then I would leave.

"Do you think it's possible to ever have a second first impression of someone?"

I looked up to see that Zach was standing in front of me with a pair of aviators on. He pulled them off and his blue eyes pierced into mine. He grabbed the chair and sat down with aplomb, giving me a wide smile. "Sorry I'm late, Piper, I'd forgotten how bad the traffic is in the Bay Area."

"You live in LA." I raised an eyebrow at him. "The traffic is way worse in LA."

"True, but I know that I always leave 30 minutes earlier back home. That was my indirect way of saying that I regret being late. Well, maybe not so indirect because I did start off saying I was sorry."

"Hi, Zach." I gave him a small smile. "It's fine."

"Knock knock."

"What?"

"Knock knock." He gave me a knowing look.

"Who's there?" I asked reluctantly.

"Amos."

"Amos who?"

"A mosquito just bit me." He grinned, but I didn't respond. "Knock knock." he said again.

"Really?"

"Knock knock."

"Who's there?" I rolled my eyes.

"Andy."

"Andy who?"

"And he just bit me again." He laughed this time and leaned forward across the cedarwood table.

"Funny," I said with a small smile.

"I'd rather it was you, though."

"You'd rather what was me?"

"I'd rather it was you that had bitten me twice. Even one time would do. Or three. Or ten." He winked at me and I just shook my head at him, even though my insides were warming up.

"No disguise today, Jethro?"

"The aviators are enough." He shrugged. "Everyone in SF is too cool for school, no one cares about me."

"I don't know about that. There are a lot of rich people, but they're nerds. Trust me, they care."

"Well, it's a good thing I had a driver drop me off right outside the door. Cool bar. Do you come here often?"

"That sounds like a pickup line."

"Maybe I'm trying to pick you up, hmmm? Have you considered that?"

"Can you pick someone up that you've already had sex with?" I laughed then and he grabbed my hands and squeezed my fingers.

"Thanks for meeting up with me. I'm sorry for how I ended things."

"You mean throwing $2000 at me?" I gave him my angriest stare.

"Yes," He sighed deeply. "That wasn't my proudest moment."

"I agree. I'm worth a lot more than $2000." I said with a small wink and he dropped my hands and leaned back and started laughing harder than I'd ever seen him laugh before. "What's so funny? You don't think I'm worth more?"

"I'm not laughing at you. I think you're worth way more than $2000. I'm just surprised that you're even talking to me and joking with me. I didn't expect you to be so nice."

"Nice? Is that a word that means anything?" I said, but I knew what he meant. I had surprised myself as well. I hadn't planned on even smiling at him.

"Hey, I'm Sarah. Did you guys have a chance to look at the menus yet or do you need a minute?"

"Can we have a moment?" I said with a small smile. She nodded and backed away. "Do you want to get a drink?"

"I do. Is the food here good?"

"As good as you can get at an Irish Pub that's not in Ireland."

"What are you getting to eat?"

"Is that really what you came here to talk about, Zach?" I folded my hands and leaned forward on the table. I wasn't going to let him flirt his way out of this one. Something about him that just made me enjoy being around him. I felt a lightness around him that I hadn't felt in years, and that scared me. I didn't like someone having power over me like that, especially him. He had too much power to hurt me, he already had and I didn't want to be hurt anymore. I had way too much going on in my life for that.

"No," he stood up and then he got down on his knees and

stared up at me. My heart was thudding now, racing so fast that I thought that I was going to have a heart attack. There was no way that he was going to propose, was there? Oh God, I could feel myself starting to panic. What if he proposed? I mean he was an actor. Didn't they call it Hollyweird? Didn't actors get married really quickly sometimes?

"Zach, I uh, I—"

"Piper, will you—"

"No, I can't, Zach. This is way too much too fast. We seriously do not even know each other."

"What?" He blinked up at me, looking confused, and then he started laughing. "Oh no, did you think I was about to propose?"

"Weren't you?"

"Nooooooo, I was just asking you to forgive me in the most dramatic way known to man." He jumped up off of his feet, a huge smile on his face. "But it's good to know that you weren't going to say yes."

"Who would say yes in this position?"

"A gold digger." He held his hands up. "Not that I'm calling you a golddigger. I'm just saying that a gold digger would have been all up on me ..." He stopped talking then and just made a face. "I'm not making it better, am I?"

"You're not making it worse," I said wryly.

"I'm on the bottom rung already, huh?"

"No, not really." I shrugged, not wanting to smile, but not being able to stop myself. "To be honest—"

But before I could finish my sentence, three women approached the table, talking loudly

"Oh my gosh, oh my gosh, is that you, Oracle Lion? Oh my gosh, Joanie, it's Oracle Lion." A lady with short dark hair and a Greenbay Packers sweater started squealing as she interrupted my conversation with Zach. "We love you,

Oracle! We love the *Babymaker* movies. Oh my gosh, you're so hot."

She was giggling as she talked to him and the other two women were staring at each other with gobsmacked expressions while reaching for their cellphones.

"Hi Oracle, I'm Katie, Katie Jones. We're here in San Fran visiting from Wisconsin. This is my sister, Joanie, and that's my friend Mickey. She's the one that was just talking to you. Can we get your autograph? We are legit your biggest fans."

I stared at the conversation in amusement. Zach didn't look fazed in the least, and I imagined that this was what he had to deal with on a daily basis. No wonder he'd been dressed up in the cupcake store that first day I'd met him.

"Hi, Oracle, I'm Joanie, Joanie Jones." The last girl spoke in a breathy voice and I watched as she touched him on the shoulder. She was very pretty, with long blonde hair and a short white dress on. She looked to be about twenty-two, and I was very jealous when I noticed the way that Zach was smiling back at her. I recognized that smile. He'd given me the same smile a couple of times when he was trying to charm me.

"Nice to make your acquaintance, ladies, I'm Oracle Lion." He winked at them, and they all practically swooned. "Would you like a drink? It's the least I could do for three Wisconsin women. I'm going to guess you pretty ladies would all like a beer?"

He stood up then and gave me a little shrug before turning his attention back to them. I sat there feeling uncomfortable and foolish. Just a minute ago, I'd been joking around and contemplating sleeping with him again, already having forgotten how rude he'd been to me and the questions Alexa wanted me to ask him, and now he was flirting it up with a bunch of skanks who hadn't even had the courtesy to acknowledge me at all. Granted,

I knew that they couldn't care less about me, and Zach had to be friendly to his fans, but for him to be so dismissive of me and to offer them a drink? *Hell no!* I wasn't putting up with that.

I'd given him a second chance and he had blown it once again. I watched Oracle and the ladies walk to the bar, and then I stood up and left the bar. I wondered how long it would take for Oracle to realize that I'd gone.

CHAPTER 15

ZACH

"ORACLE LION, will you sign an autograph for me?" One of my fans pushed her breasts up against my arm and batted her eyelashes up at me.

"Sure, what's your name, sweetie?"

"I already told you, it's Joanie." She pouted and I chuckled as her name left my brain again. I waited for the bartender to bring over the three beers and it suddenly struck me that I hadn't asked Piper what she wanted to drink. I looked towards the table to call her over to the bar, but the table was empty. I frowned and took a step forward to look around the bar. Maybe she'd changed tables. I still couldn't see her, though. I walked over to the table we'd been sitting at but there was nothing there except her empty water glass.

"Oracle, what are you doing?" The three girls followed me back to the table, each one holding a beer in her hand. "Joanie just ordered us shots of whiskey." They stopped next to me, but my attention had gone from them completely. I looked around the bar, my heart racing, and tried to figure out where Piper had gone.

"The girl you were here with left, mate," one of the guys that had been seated at the table next to us called out. "You showed up late and then left with three other women, I think she's had enough."

"Thanks." I pursed my lips and sighed. Why had Piper just left? This was my life. I had to be nice to fans. Didn't she understand that? Every other woman I'd gone out with had understood and known to just take care of themselves when situations like this happened. I pulled out my phone and was about to text Piper when I changed my mind and called her. This was a time when a call was needed over a text.

The phone rang and rang and went to voicemail and I let out a huge sigh as I hung up and rushed to the front of the bar and the street to see if I could see Piper outside. Maybe she'd just been trying to make a statement. She wouldn't have actually left, would she?

"Want to come back to our hotel, Oracle?" One of the women had followed me and was now whispering in my ear, and I shook my head. "I've heard you're a wild boy. Why don't you show us?"

"Not tonight." I dialed Piper's number again and started pacing back and forth.

"Watch where you're going, asshole!" a man shouted through a car window as he slowed down next to me. "I nearly ran over your foot."

I looked up at him in surprise, not having realized I had walked into the road. "Sor—" I started to say, but he drove off before I could finish.

I walked back to the pavement and took a seat at one of the small round tables outside the pub. The woman who had whispered in my ear hovered near me but I just completely ignored her. I didn't have time for this bullshit. How could

Piper just leave? She hadn't even said goodbye. I called her number again and clenched the phone tightly.

"Stop calling me!" she snapped.

I breathed a sigh of relief that at least she'd answered. There was no way I was leaving San Francisco without having a real conversation with her.

"You just left," I said accusingly. "How could you do that?"

"Actually, I think *you're* the one who just left," she retorted. "We were sitting at a table chatting and you just got up and left me."

"I was just trying to be nice to fans. That's a part of my job."

"That's good for you, but you already disrespected my time when you showed up late. I wasn't about to just sit there and wait for you to return to me when you were done flirting up a storm."

"No one else I know has a problem with me being friendly to fans."

"Don't try and twist this, Zach, or should I say, *Oracle Lion*." She took a deep breath. "Look, whatever. You have to do you, but I don't have to stick around and be a witness to that. I have a life."

"Don't hang up, please," I said, trying to process what she'd said.

Didn't she know that I was THE Oracle Lion? That I had duties to my fans? Why couldn't she just accept that? No other woman had ever complained to me, let alone walked out. But for some strange reason that made me like her more.

"I didn't intend to be rude. I'm sorry. I was lucky that you even agreed to meet up with me again, I know that."

"Yeah, well, it seems like you don't intend to be rude a lot. But almost every time I've met you, you've been rude as hell."

"Not in the cupcake shop, though."

"Yeah, maybe not there." She sighed. "Look, I gotta go. I'm hungry, and I need to find something to eat."

"Can I buy you dinner and we can talk about your historical romance book and what you're working on now?"

"Why did you even read the book?" She sounded nonplussed. "Doesn't seem your style."

"Heaving bosoms are always my style."

That got a small laugh out of her. "Zach, you're a typical bro. Were you in a fraternity when you were in college?"

"Actually, yes, Delta Upsilon. I pledged with my two best friends."

I froze. I'd nearly slipped up by talking about Radley and Jackson. I'd already forgotten the main reason for me coming to see her, forgotten as soon as I'd seen her beautiful face there in the bar, waiting for me. It was strange how I felt when I saw her and talked to her. We bantered like we'd known each other for years, and when I touched her skin, I felt like I was a part of something real. It was hard to explain, even to myself, but being around Piper made me feel alive in a way I'd never felt before.

"Two best friends?" She asked lightly, but there was a slight change in her voice. "Jackson and who?"

"So can I see you?" I cut her off. "Please?"

"Maybe. It depends." She hesitated and then continued. "I'll meet up with you if you let me ask you a few questions."

"A few questions?" My blood chilled. So she was writing a book about me. All of my hope and excitement dulled as I resigned myself to the fact that Piper was just another leech trying to drain me of something. I bet her leaving the pub had been a part of her game in trying to get me to come to her.

"Yeah, a few questions." She sighed. "It's not really for me, but it would mean a lot."

"I'll answer a few questions if you play a game with me."

"What game?"

"Truth or dare."

"Truth or dare?"

"I'll always pick truth so that you can ask me your questions, but you have to always answer dare, and I will only answer as many questions as dares that you take and ..."

"There's more?" she interrupted me, sounding nervous.

"Yes, there's more. One last caveat." I paused for dramatic effect.

"And that is?"

"You have to go first."

"That's not fair," she protested. "Why do I go first?"

"So I know you're going to follow through with the dares if I answer the questions." I grinned into the phone, thinking of all the things I was going to have her do. If she was going to play me, I might as well have a good time. "Don't worry, we'll go back and forth. I'll make sure that we make it fair. So what do you say, Piper, are you game?"

"Game on, Zach. The game is on. Where shall we meet?"

I decided to try and push my luck and see if she would bite. "I have a suite at the Hotel Fairmont, meet me there?"

"But what about dinner?"

"I'm your dinner," I growled into the phone, and then because I didn't want her to take me too seriously, I added, "We can order room service or eat in the restaurant."

"I think I'll choose the restaurant, thanks."

"So then I'll see you there in fifteen minutes?"

"Sure. And I'm warning you, there is no third chance. You screw this up and I'm out."

"I won't screw it up," I said with a laugh. "But that doesn't mean I won't screw you," I said under my breath.

I wasn't sure if she'd heard that last part because she'd already hung up. She sure did have a thing about getting off of the phone quickly, and that annoyed me. Normally, I couldn't get a woman off of the phone fast enough, but that wasn't the case with Piper. In fact, she hadn't even asked me if I'd given her a burner number like most women did. To be honest, I hadn't even thought about calling from one of my pay-as-you-go phones. Maybe I'd been blinded by her smile and her wit, but Piper Meadows had very much gotten under my skin. If she wanted information from me, I was going to make her pay. I was going to make sure that by the end of the night, I was under her skin as well, and it wasn't just going to be all about her questions. Oh no, I had other plans. Plans that were going to make her regret having ever tried to play me.

CHAPTER 16

PIPER

FLY ME TO THE MOON. Let me play among the stars.

Frank Sinatra's voice carried through the hotel lobby, and I bobbed my head slightly to the familiar tune. "In other words, baby, kiss me," I sang along under my breath.

"You made it." I felt a hand on my back and looked up into Zach's familiar blue eyes. "I was beginning to think you weren't going to make it."

"You've been waiting for me?"

"All my life," he said and my heart stopped for a second. What did that mean? "Do you want to dance?"

"Dance?" I looked at him in surprise. "Where's the dance floor?"

"Right here."

He grasped my hands, pulled me close, and we glided gracefully across the lobby. I could see guests and hotel staff staring at us, but no one came to stop us. Most probably because the hotel manager knew he was Oracle Lion. The whispering became louder and people were gasping and muttering excitedly as they realized that a real-life star was in their hotel lobby. My cheeks were tinged with pink at everyone staring at us, but Zach paid them no attention.

"Focus on me," he said as his hand slid to the small of my back. His eyes were intense as he stared at me and I nodded slightly, enjoying the feel of his body against mine. "Do you enjoy dancing?" he asked softly as he brought me in closer to him.

"Yes, but normally in the privacy of my home or a dark, packed club."

My fingers were tingling at his touch, and I could feel the warmth of his body permeating me. He guided me around the room, his legs brushing past mine, and I could feel the tightness of his muscles. My breasts pressed into his chest and my right hand rested on his shoulder.

After a few minutes of dancing, I'd forgotten that there was anyone else in the hotel aside from us. His eyes never left mine, and it almost felt like we were making love. Zach was a smooth, precise dancer, and when he started singing along with the Patsy Cline's "Crazy," I could feel my legs shaking. He sang soulfully and I just stared up at him in admiration. What could this guy not do?

"I love that song."

"Did you know that it was written by Willie Nelson?"

"The Willie Nelson?"

"Yup." He grinned. "He wrote the song in 1961, and Patsy Cline released it in 1962."

"You know a lot about Patsy Cline," I said in surprise. "I thought you used to be in a rock band with Jackson?"

"I did."

"But you know all about country music?"

"I grew up in the South." He shrugged. "And I like country music. Also, this was one of my dad's favorite songs."

"Oh?"

"And subsequently it became one of my mom's favorite songs. She used to sing it to me every night when I was a child."

"Really?" I looked at him as his eyes had glazed over in memories. "That's a weird song to sing to your child."

"Yes, it is, isn't it?" He nodded as he looked back down at me with a wry smile. "But that's my mom."

"Are your parents still in the South?"

"Mom lives in Florida still. My dad is dead."

"Oh, I'm sorry." I squeezed his hand. I didn't know what was happening between us. There was a weird crazy sort of connection that we had that I'd never felt with anyone else. It almost felt like we'd known each other for years. No matter how mad I was, whenever I saw him, those feelings all fled.

"Nothing for you to be sorry about. Have you ever heard the song, "Have You Ever Seen The Rain?" He asked me, changing the subject. "The version with Willie Nelson with his daughter, Paula Nelson?"

"No, I don't think so."

"It's beautiful. Sometimes when I go surfing at night, I'll listen to it on the car radio before I head into the water."

"Oh, wow, really?"

"Yeah." He nodded. "You know we should go to a Willie Nelson concert together sometime."

"You'd be mobbed."

"I'm good at disguises, remember?"

"Yeah, I remember." I shivered as I felt his hand on my ass. He rubbed it gently and I could feel the spot heating up. "So want to go?"

"I don't know." I didn't know how to answer him. Was he asking me seriously? And if so what did that mean? He wanted to see me again? Why? He was such an enigma.

"He performs with many of his kids. I think it's great to see a family of performers."

"Yeah, I had no idea." I didn't want to admit that the only Willie Nelson song I knew was *On the Road Again* and that was because it had been part of Guitar Hero. "You know a lot about him and his family. You sound like one of his biggest fans."

"I've been approached to play a young Willie Nelson in a biopic." He admitted with a boyish smile. "I'm considering it."

"Wow, that would be cool." I said, impressed. "I saw the Freddie Mercury movie, *Bohemian Rhapsody*. It was really good."

"It wasn't bad." He suddenly stopped dancing and leaned forward and kissed me. I was taken aback at the feel of his lips on mine but I kissed him back wantonly, moving my hands up to his neck and then running my fingers through his hair. I could feel his cock throbbing next to my belly, and I swallowed hard.

"I want to be in your warm pussy right now," he whispered against my lips, his eyes shining wickedly into mine. "I can almost taste you on my tongue."

He kissed me hard one more time before grabbing my hand and pulling me along with him. I followed behind him dazed and barely able to think as the crowds of people clapped for us.

"That's going to be on TMZ within the next couple of hours, what do you want to bet?" He sighed and gave me an apologetic look. "Sorry about that. I wasn't thinking about people."

"But don't you always get recognized and photographed?" I thought back to the bar earlier in the evening.

"Yes, but I was only thinking of dancing with you, not anything else. You made me forget who I was for a few minutes there." We stopped in front of the elevator and he smiled as he pressed the button. "I hope you don't mind, but we're going to my room. We can order room service, okay?"

"That's fine," I said, not even bothering to push the issue. The last place I wanted to be was in the restaurant right now. I wanted to feel his tongue in places that would make me forget my name.

"I like your skirt." He moved closer to me. "It's sexy, like you."

"Thank you," I said with a shy smile. What was he playing at? Another couple was standing right next to us. He shifted even closer to me and ran a finger down my cheek.

"You have so many secrets in your eyes, don't you?"

"I wouldn't say I have many secrets, no." I reached up and ran my fingers down his chest and all the way down to his belt. "But I do think you have many, many, secrets."

"Secrets that you want to know about?"

"Perhaps," I said, and his eyes darkened. "Are you going to tell me?"

"Are you going to ask me those questions?"

"If you'll give me answers."

"Did you know that the ocean is full of secrets? There are no lies. No truths. No imperfections. The ocean is life, is love, is me. My surfboard is my guide. The waves are my master. And all the answers you seek are found in her depths."

"You're telling me to ask my questions to the ocean? Or is that some sort of riddle?"

"No riddle." His eyes had that distant light again. "I just love the ocean."

The bell dinged then to let us know that the elevator had arrived and he stepped to the side to let me enter first. We walked in, and I waited for the couple to join us, but they didn't and the doors closed.

"Okay, are you ready?" He pressed the button to the top floor and then faced me.

"Ready for what?"

"Your first dare."

"My first dare?" I swallowed hard. "What's the dare?"

"Take off your panties and give them to me."

"What? Here?" My jaw dropped, but I have to admit that I was turned on as well.

"Yes, here." He nodded. "If you have any questions you want me to answer, you need to fulfill dare number one."

"Or?"

"Or you get no answers to any questions." His lips curled up. "Your choice."

He stood there staring at me, and I knew that he thought I didn't have it in me. He thought I was too meek or shy to take off my panties. And he was right—I was freaking out inside. Who took off their panties in an elevator in a public hotel? I wasn't even drunk. But then something came over me. I wanted to take that smirk and smug look off of his face. I quickly slipped my black heels off and handed them to him.

"Hold these," I ordered.

He raised an eyebrow. "These aren't your panties," he said as he held them up.

"Oh, trust me, I know." This time I gave him the smirk. I lifted my skirt off and pulled my black thong off slowly and held it on the tip of my finger. I walked over to Zach and waved the thong in front of his eyes, then placed it in his pocket. Then, because I wanted to shock him even more, I grabbed his hand and placed it under my skirt, right next to my wetness. I guided his fingers along my clit and trembled as his fingers started to rub me gently. With a growl, Zach pushed me back up against the wall of the elevator and kissed the side of my neck. I closed my eyes and began to moan as he slipped a finger inside of me. His lips met mine again and we kissed with abandon, his tongue entering my mouth as one hand continued to finger me.

"You're so wet for me, you naughty girl," he growled then we both jumped in shock when the elevator stopped. "Stand in front of me." He whispered as he removed his hand from under my skirt. A handsome older man and what appeared to be his son gave us a quick nod and stood on the other side of the elevator. They pressed the 20th floor and the doors closed.

Zach's hands went around my waist and then he pulled me back into him. I could feel his hardness pressing into me and I wiggled my ass back against him slightly. I heard his sharp intake of breath and grinned.

"Wait, are you Oracle Lion?" the younger man suddenly said as he looked over at us again in the elevator, his eyes wide and excited.

"Indeed I am."

"Can I get your autograph?"

"Sorry, not tonight." Oracle's voice was regretful. "I'm dedicating this night to—" His voice broke off as the elevator stopped and the light flickered. I let out a small shriek in fright as we were plunged into darkness.

The younger man speaking again. "What the hell?" He sounded angry. "How can a hotel as expensive as this one have a faulty elevator?"

"Just calm down, Lucas. It will be fine," the older man answered him.

"Mom is going to be wondering where we are." So I'd been right.

"She's watching that bachelor show on TV, and she's on the phone with your Aunt Sheila. She won't even notice we're gone."

I smiled at his comment, but then stilled when I felt Zach's hand creeping up under my top and over my bra. He

J. S. COOPER

slipped his fingers into my bra cup and gently pinched my nipples. I bit down on my lower lip to stop myself from moaning or crying out.

"Lean forward," he whispered in my ear, but I didn't move.

He chuckled in my ear lightly and then lifted the back of my skirt up and started rubbing my ass. I wasn't sure if I heard or felt the sound of his zip going down but the next thing I knew I was feeling the head of his cock between my ass cheeks. His fingers left my bra and moved down between my legs and started rubbing my clit again. My legs started trembling at his touch and I reached behind to steady myself.

"Lean forward," he whispered in my ear again and rubbed on my clit more urgently.

This time I obeyed and bent forward slightly in the darkness. I couldn't believe what we were doing right here in the elevator. An elevator that held two other people. Two other people who were probably wondering what all the whispering was about. Two people that would see us in a compromising position if the lights came back on as quickly as they'd turned off. I knew all of this, but still I didn't care. I think part of the situation was what made it even more exciting. Zach removed his fingers from my wetness and guided the tip of his cock to my opening. He rubbed it back and forth along my clit for a few seconds before entering me.

"Ahhh!" I cried out as I felt the full length of his cock inside of me.

"Are you okay?" the older man asked me in the dark. "There's no need to be scared, I'm sure they will have us out soon."

"I'm okay, thanks," I squeaked out, almost moaning again as Zach moved his cock slowly inside of me. And then he increased his pace and if I hadn't been in so much ecstasy, I would have worried about the noise his cock was making as it slid in and out of my pussy.

Zach was harder than I'd thought he would have been given our lack of foreplay, but I suppose the situation turned him on as well. He grabbed my hips and moved me back into him and I circled my hips as I bounced my ass back against him every time he slammed into me. I was so close to coming and I was scared I was going to scream so I stuffed part of my top into my mouth. I could hear Zach breathing harder and I was nervous the two men knew what was going on. The elevator was pretty silent asides from the small noises we were making, but I wasn't sure if we were really being loud or if the sounds were being amplified in my head. I was just about to come and then I felt him pulling out of me completely. I wanted to cry at the loss of his cock inside of me, but I knew I couldn't say anything.

"I don't have on a rubber," he whispered in my ear as he pulled me back up and dropped the back of my skirt back down.

I could have slapped myself for my idiocy. t that I hadn't even thought about protection. Shit, if he hadn't pulled out, he would have come inside of me and that could have ended up being a whole heap of drama. I didn't say anything back to him, and I was thanking God about ten seconds later that he'd pulled out because the lights flickered back on and the elevator started moving again.

"See, I told you it would be okay." The older man offered me a fatherly smile and I just smiled back at him weakly, unable to say anything. The elevator stopped at the 20th floor and the two men got out. Zach turned me around to face him, a huge smile on his face.

"That was fucking hot." He pulled me towards him and kissed me hard. "I can't wait to get to the room to finish what we started."

"Don't I get my question first?" I teased him, not giving a hoot about asking any questions. All I wanted was for him to finish what he'd started. I needed his cock inside of me again, and I needed to climax. I was all worked up and I needed a release.

"You can ask all the questions you want afterwards."

He lifted up my top and then pulled my bra down slightly. Taking my right breast into his mouth, he sucked on my nipple while his fingers started playing with my clit again.

"You're so wet for me."

He fingered me and I could tell that I was going to come. I moaned and squeezed my legs together and he must have realized what was happening because the next thing I knew he was lifting me up against the wall.

"Wrap your legs around my waist," he commanded me and I did so eagerly. He unzipped his pants again and pulled his cock out. And placed it at my entrance.

"But you have no condom," I said looking at him.

"Don't worry." He kissed my lips and grinned. "I can control myself. I want to feel you coming on my dick. Right now. In this elevator," he said and then he entered me.

I bit down on his shoulder as he thrust into me, my pussy closing on his cock like it never wanted to be without him again. "Come for me, Piper, come for me."

He kissed me hard and rotated his hips so that his cock was hitting me in a different spot. Then he moved his fingers down to my clit and rubbed me as well and I felt the waves come crashing down as I climaxed hard. He groaned as my body trembled against the wall and I held onto him tight. He thrust into me a few more times and then pulled out with a small smile. "That's about as much control as I have right now," he said.

When the elevator stopped again, and we practically ran to his room and I waited for him to open the door.

"Nice room," I said as I looked around briefly, but Zach didn't have time for that. He was ripping his clothes off and then mine and placing me on the bed. He buried his head between my legs and I felt his tongue licking up all my juices.

"You taste so good," he said as he kissed back up to my lips. "Now it's my turn."

"Do you have a condom?"

"Yes."

He reached over to the side table and pulled a wrapper off of it, ripped it open and slipped it on.

"Get on your knees," he said and then came up behind me. I leaned forward and placed my hands in front of me and felt him entering me from behind in one long, deep stroke. He slammed into me with abandon, while reaching around me and grabbing my breasts. It was only a couple of minutes later that I felt him shuddering inside of me and then sliding out of me. We both fell back on the bed, panting deeply and he reached over and touched my hair lightly.

"So ... it's good seeing you again," he said wryly. "Thanks for giving me a third chance."

"Uh huh," I said with a small smile and reached over to touch his face. "You're a very lucky man."

"Yes, I am." He lightly traced a hand across my stomach. "I haven't forgotten that I still owe you dinner."

"Yes, you do. I'm starved," I said, and with that, he reached over, grabbed a room service menu and handed it to me.

"I HAVEN'T HAD such a delicious burger and fries in a while." I happily licked the last remnants of salt from my fingers. "That really hit the spot."

"Yes, my cock did seem to hit several spots, didn't it?" He

watched me as I ate in my big white towel robe on top of the bed. He was seated naked in the chair opposite the bed, just staring at me. "I've never seen a woman eat so voraciously," He said as I put my plate down on the side table.

"Maybe that's because you live in LA?" I said with a small shrug. "I'm a writer, no one cares if I'm as skinny as a pencil, so I can actually enjoy food."

"Skinny as a pencil, ha." He laughed. "I'm glad you're not as skinny as a pencil." He licked his lips and I could see his cock growing.

"So now I wanted to ask you some questions." I took a deep breath. This hadn't quite gone the way that I'd expected. I hadn't wanted to have sex with him again, and I certainly didn't expect to be asking him what could potentially be hard-hitting questions from his bed dressed in nothing but a hotel robe.

"Okay," he leaned forward, his eyes narrowing. "Getting down to business, I see."

"You have to be honest."

"I'll be honest," he said as he stood up tall and I stared at his gloriously tall and strong muscular body.

It suddenly struck me just how fit he was—beyond just being sexy, I mean. If things got ugly, there was no way that I'd be able to take him down and leave. I really was a dumbass. Had I put myself in danger for some love-making? Granted, it was the best sex I'd ever had in my life, but was it worth it now that he defintely was in a position of power over me? I was really nervous right now. What if I found out something I didn't want to know?

"First, let me say a few things," he said as he made his way over to the bed and lay down on the mattress. He leaned forward and untied my belt. My robe fell open. He took in the sight of my naked body and smiled. "Take your robe off," he ordered, but I just sat there. "Take it off, Piper."

"What if I don't want to?"

"Oh, but you do. You very much want to take it off," he said, his eyes gazing into mine and daring me to argue with him.

"I don't really care either way," I said cooly as I slipped the robe off. The game of cat and mouse had started, and I needed to let him know who was boss. "Though I should call Alexa in a little bit. She knows I'm here at the Fairmont with you, and I don't want her to worry as I didn't tell her I'd be spending the night."

"I don't think she'll be staying up the night waiting for you to get home."

"She worries."

"I bet she's already in bed."

"If I don't make it home by a certain time, she will likely call the police. She's over-dramatic like that."

"There are many places we could be by that time happens."

"If I'm not back home by morning, she'll panic. She knows I have a deadline."

"For your book, huh?"

"Yes." I nodded and swallowed hard.

"It would be a pity if you weren't able to finish that book, wouldn't it?"

"I guess so." I shrugged, looking away nonchalantly. I was not going to tell him about vampires falling in love right now. He'd laugh me off of the bed.

"I could whisk you away before that could ever happen."

"Against my will?"

"Would it really be against your will, though?" His finger stroked my shoulder and his eyes stared into mine hard. I shivered at the look on his face. This was no intimate gaze. This was a hard, searching look. What had he done? And was he aware that I might know?

"I want you to tell me about Radley Markham," I said, finally cutting to the chase. I'd intended to skirt around the issue to catch him unawares, but I needed the element of surprise.

His face twisted, and for a second, I saw a flash of sadness in his gaze. The room was silent, save for our breathing, as we both sat there. I stared at his eyes, his lips, his hands, hands that had just made me come in the most magnificent of ways, and I wanted to believe that somehow Alexa had gotten it wrong. I wanted to believe that Zach had nothing to do with Radley. Maybe it hadn't even been him in the photo. Or Jackson. Maybe he had never met him.

"Zach?" I prompted.

"What do you want to know?" His voice was bleak, and my heart sank.

"Did you have anything to do with Radley Markham's disappearance?" I asked the question I cared about most and then wondered if I should have led with what Spacecoast69 had mentioned.

"So it's true." He sighed. He reached forward and touched my lips gently and shook his head. "I tried to tell myself it wasn't true, but it's true. You should have been an actress in Hollywood, Piper, you really should."

"Don't change the subject, Zach. I want to know." I swallowed hard, and I knew my body was flushed with anxiety. If this went badly, I was going to be all alone. I had lied earlier. Alexa didn't know I was here at the Fairmont. She'd known I was heading to Kells to meet Zach, yes, but when I'd left, I hadn't told her anything. I hadn't wanted her to get upset.

"Yes, Piper, I had something to do with Radley Markham's disappearance."

My heart stopped. I couldn't quite believe it. "What happened?" I asked, trying to make sure I didn't directly ask him if he'd killed him.

"If I give you this information, you need to do something for me."

"What?"

"You need to call Alexa right now and tell her you're not coming home."

"Not coming home?" I blinked at him. "What?"

"That's all I'm going to say for now."

"What if I want to leave?"

"You're not going to leave now, Piper. So I'm going to have you call Alexa and tell her that you're not coming home."

"Are you going to hurt me?" I whispered.

"I would never hurt you, Piper." He traced a finger down my cheek. "Never."

"So why do I have to call Alexa?"

"If I tell you what I'm going to tell you, then I can't have you leaving me ... right away." He added on the last words and I wondered if they were there to make me feel better. Was he ever going to let me leave?

"I don't know."

He pushed me back onto the bed and kissed down my neck and along my collarbone as his right hand fondled my breasts. I couldn't breathe and I couldn't tell him to stop. I didn't want to. The danger in the air was palpable, but so was the sex. I wanted him in ways that I'd never wanted anyone before and I was feeling things that I shouldn't be. I didn't even recognize myself. Zach Houston had me like a puppet on strings. I couldn't move as I waited to see what he was going to do next.

"I want to fuck you again," he said against my mouth, biting down on my lower lip a little too hard before sucking it into his mouth. "I want to hear you screaming my name. You're going to be mine, Piper. You're going to do exactly what I want, do you hear?"

"I hear you," I said as my fingers ran down his back. "But

what I don't hear is you answering my question. That was the deal, Zach. I want to know."

"You want to know, eh?" He hovered over me, his cock resting on my stomach, growing harder with each second. I reached down to stroke it and he growled against my mouth, his eyes seeming to stare into my soul. "I'll tell you everything you want to know, Piper." He kissed along my jawbone to my ear and then whispered. "I was with Radley on the night that he disappeared, and I know exactly what happened. I know because I'm the one that did it."

The End

READY TO FIND out what happens next? Secrets of the Playboy is the sequel to The Playboy and will be out in three weeks. Join my mailing list here to ensure you don't miss this explosive finale. Everything you think you know will be called into question. Can you guess Zach's secrets?

READY TO READ another J. S. Cooper book right now? Don't worry, I've got many more sexy fun books for you to read!

ALONG CAME BABY

I just wanted to have some fun...

It all started when I moved into my new apartment in Brooklyn and met my neighbor, Olivia. We became fast friends and so when she had to go out of town on an emergency work trip, I agreed to give her brother her keys so he could look after her dog. And then I met him. Her brother was Carter Stevens and he was sex on legs. He was a banker by day and a musician by night; arrogant, handsome, with the most tantalizing smile I'd ever seen. When he invited me to his show, I couldn't say no.

HE WASN'T LOOKING for a relationship...

The night of the show we stumbled back to my place and had fun I can only blush thinking about. I'd never had a one-night stand before, but one night soon led to two, which led to three. Carter was exciting and mysterious, but he was a total playboy. He made it clear that this was some no strings attached fun.

BUT FATE HAD other plans for us...

I thought we'd been careful, but I guess there was that one time that we weren't. And now, I'm pregnant and Carter Stevens and I have to figure out what to do next because one thing we both know for sure is that the baby is coming in nine months and we have no idea what to do next.

READ ALONG CAME BABY NOW.

DANTE

A BLIND DATE set up by her grandmothers best friend.
    A mistaken identity.
    A crying baby left at her apartment.

WHAT COULD POSSIBLY GO wrong for Sadie Johnson? Just

about everything. She thought her week couldn't get any worse and then she went on her date and met Dante.

DANTE VANDERBILT. Hot, charming, sexy, rich, and arrogant. He was the sort of man that every woman wanted to tame. Every woman except Sadie. She disliked him on sight and she let him know that right away. However that only seemed to amuse him and want her even more. Even though he assumed she was a flighty, careless single mother. Even though she let him believe that was true and that she would never want him as a stepdad to her pretend kid. He seemed to find her distaste appealing which only irritated her even more. Sadie couldn't wait to leave the date and Dante behind, only he seemed to keep popping up wherever she went.

SADIE WASN'T sure what Dante wanted from her, but one thing she knew for sure was that she was in way over her head.

READ DANTE NOW.

FILTHY LITTLE LIES
He's The Man of My Dreams
I met a man and I can't tell anyone who he is. I shouldn't tell you about the things we do. The things he does to me. The things I do to him. I shouldn't tell you that he's the love of my life. The sex is hot; the romance is real; the love is explosive, and the lies will shatter everything in both of our lives.

. . .

He Doesn't Know I Have a Secret

You see, he doesn't really know who I am. And I found out I don't really know who he is. We both have secrets. We both have hidden desires. And we're both about to go on the roller coaster ride of our lives.

Read Filthy Little Lies Now.

One Night Stand

It was only supposed to be one night!

We met at a wedding. He was hot. And I'd been in a year's drought.

He smiled. We got drunk. We flirted. We hooked up. I left early the next morning without saying goodbye. It was only meant to be a one night stand. I didn't want the awkward morning after moment. Not at all.

Then I went home for the weekend. And he was there. Sitting on the couch chatting to my dad. Turns out he was more than just a stranger. Turns out that my one night stand was about to cause a whole heap of trouble. Turns out that it never just stops with one night.

Read One Night Stand Now.

. . .

The Ex Games

Secrets, lies, and lust collide in The Ex Games as a billionaire and the woman he's not willing to let go have to figure out just how willing they are to play.

She started it.

Just one little secret was all it took to shatter my trust, to destroy our relationship. I thought Katie Raymond was the one. All of my money couldn't have bought a better future than one that had her beautiful face in it.

That was then. Now, the secret is mine. And once she realizes I'm the new owner of her company, the ball will be in my court.

But it isn't my only secret.

This time, I'm the one who's been lying.

He finished me.

Handsome and charming, Brandon Hastings was my first romance, my first love. With his body, he taught me things I never knew I needed. I never wanted to stop exploring each other.

· · ·

166

SEVEN YEARS LATER, I'm going to see him again. And this time, he's my boss.

I WON'T LET Brandon break me again.

I ONLY WISH my body would stop betraying me every time he walks into a room.

SEVEN YEARS AGO, I made the biggest mistake of my life by not opening up to the man I loved. It cost me everything.

I THOUGHT I was done paying.

I HAD no idea how deep the secrets went.

GAME OVER.

READ THE EX GAMES NOW.

STAY IN TOUCH

Stay up-to-date with my books by signing up for my newsletter.

Follow J. S. Cooper online:

Instagram

Facebook

Mailing List

Email me at jscooperauthor@gmail.com

EXCERPT FROM ONE NIGHT STAND

"YOU CAN STILL CALL ME MR. TONGUE, IF YOU WANT." HE grinned at me and licked his lips deliberately, the tip of his tongue gliding back and forth, reminding me of the night we'd spent together—the sinful night that I'd never forget. Only he wasn't supposed to be here. In my parents' house. Sitting on my couch. The couch I'd watched TV on for years. He wasn't supposed to be talking to my parents. He wasn't supposed to be looking so sexy. I didn't even know his name.

One-night stands are meant to be fun. They're meant to be exciting. They're meant to be adventurous experiments in lovemaking that don't follow you home. I don't consider myself a whore or cheap. I mean, I have standards for the guys I want to date and hook up with. I even have a chart of things I look for in a guy. I don't just drop my panties for any guy with a cute smile, handsome face and a wallet full of cash. I've slept with men that had no cash, missing teeth and even one who was prematurely balding, but they were all boyfriends. Yes, I've had questionable taste in men, but that's a story for another day. One I'm not particularly proud of. In fact, I still cringe when I remember the guy with the missing teeth going down on me. It made for an unusual experience.

I know you might not believe that I have standards now. Especially considering how quickly I dropped my panties for the mysterious stranger at my friends' wedding. The mysterious stranger who was now standing in front of me. You might want to believe that I drop my panties for any man that asks, but trust me, I don't. Mr. Tongue was the exception to the rule. I dropped my panties without a second thought when I saw him. Well, actually that's a bit of a lie. *I* didn't exactly drop my panties. He took them off with his teeth. His cute, perfectly straight, sharp pearly-white teeth. Oh shit, my body can still remember his teeth grazing my skin as he pulled my white lace panties off. Honestly, in that moment, I couldn't stop him or myself. It was one of those magical moments that you see in movies. The chemistry was perfect between us; our bodies were on fire and all I could think about was him and his mouth, even though we were just one room away from a packed church. I never thought anything like that would happen to me. I got caught up in the moment. I mean, it's not every day you make eye contact with a green-eyed stranger, and he leads you to a back room in a church (God, forgive me). It's not every day that you meet a man: a gorgeous, sexy, virile stud of a man, and okay, yes he was slightly obnoxious, but I didn't care. It's not every day a hot stud has got you on the floor, with your dress riding up around your waist as he pulls your panties off with his teeth. And let's not forget his tongue. Oh my God, his tongue did things to me that I cannot repeat. Things I didn't even know existed. Like multiple orgasms in minutes—yes, I said minutes. Like one right after the other. And all from his tongue: pink, long and extremely flexible. Who knew tongues could be so flexible? Not me. And of course, he knew he'd blown my world. The grin on his face and the glint in his eye told me that he knew he was the shit. Smug, cocky bastard. As I stared at him in front of me, I knew that he could still remember that day as well. I could see it in the glint of his eye as I tried to keep my breathing under control. What had he done to me then, and why was he here now?

I'd only been slightly embarrassed as I'd climaxed on his mouth. The way he'd eagerly licked up my juices from his lips had made me feel slightly dirty. I didn't care, though. I was still too busy trying to catch my breath as I jumped up from the ground, and pulled my dress back down. I started panicking as I heard the organist playing "Here Comes the Bride". I had to get back to my pew in the church quickly and that also meant panty-less as he didn't want to give them back (and yeah, I thought that was kind of hot). I know, I have no shame. I walked back into the church that day feeling like a harlot. I'd let some nameless, random smug man go down on me, right before a wedding. Who did that?

That wasn't even the worst of it. I went home with him, too. And when I say went home, I mean to his hotel suite. His very expensive, very impressive suite at the Marriott downtown (he was most probably paying my month's rent for a long weekend). We went to his hotel room and this time he used more than his tongue. And this time, I did more than lie back with my legs in the air and his face firmly planted down smack-bang in the center. It was a night of fireworks. A night of explosive sex that blew my world and everything that I thought I knew about sex. I was ruined for the next boring man I dated. No longer would I be happy with quick foreplay and some push in and out missionary action. I'd never had sex so hot and I suppose that's the beauty of one-night stands. You hook up and do all the things you're too self-conscious to normally do. Neither one of us had expectations. We didn't even exchange names. And that's why I left early the next morning and hurried out of the room, head held as high as I could as I did the walk of shame through the hotel lobby, my smeared mascara and messy hair telling my tale to everyone that viewed me.

I didn't care, though. I'd experienced the best sex of my life and with the hottest man I'd ever met. That does something to your ego. I felt like a million dollars and I was pretty sure I'd rocked his world as well. He wouldn't forget me anytime soon; especially as he had the scratch and bite marks to remind him of our night for the next few days. It didn't even matter that he'd seemed like he could be an arrogant asshole, the way he'd bossed me around the bed. I even kind of liked his take-charge alphaness. It was good in the bedroom, though I knew in everyday life, he'd annoy me, but that didn't matter. He wasn't someone I ever had to deal with again.

I was wrong, though. Because you know how life goes. When you're riding high and feeling like you're on top of everything, something always happens to bring you back down to earth. That's what happened to me this weekend when I came home to visit my parents. The weekend after the wedding when I hooked up with Mr. Tongue. Yes, my one-night stand didn't seem so hot and innocent when I turned up at my parents' house and saw him sitting on my parents' couch. Miracle Tongue or as he called himself Mr. Tongue had nearly given me a heart attack when I'd seen him sitting there in front of me on my parents' couch, sipping Earl Grey tea. The moment he looked up at me, his green eyes laughing, was a moment I'll never forget. It was the moment that stopped my heart for what seemed like minutes. It was the moment that reminded me why I'd never had a one-night stand before. I stood there for a few seconds, before he stood up and walked over to me, a huge grin on his face.

"Hello," he said and grinned at me as he reached his hand out to me. "Nice to meet you, my name is Xander."

"I'm Liv," I said softly, my face red as I shook his hand.

"Nice to meet you, Liv." His eyes teased me as my parents stood there watching us.

"You, too." I swallowed hard. What was he doing here?

"Oh, you have something on your ear." He leaned forward and brushed something off of my ear as he whispered quietly. "Now I have a name to put to the face when I think about our night together," he said and I felt the tip of his tongue on my earlobe. I pulled back in shock and glanced at him and then back at my parents.

"What are you doing here?" I asked softly, needing an answer. This was too much of a coincidence. Of course the answer wasn't the fairytale answer that I was secretly hoping for. He hadn't tracked me down because he couldn't forget me. He hadn't come to woo me. No, of course my journey into the land of one-night stands couldn't be so perfect. Of course, my journey into one-night stands ended up being one complicated mess. I should have known that for me it wouldn't be one night of fun. I should have known that one-night stands never end at one night and they always turn into a whole bunch of trouble.

"What would you like me to be doing here?" He laughed and ran his hands through his jet-black hair. Hair I knew was silky-soft to the touch. Hair that I'd grabbed and pulled. I bit my lower lip as I stood there, in shock. If I'd known the reason why he was there, I would have run away. If I'd known who he was at the wedding, I would have said no. But of course, I wasn't privy to that information. So of course my one-night stand changed everything I thought I knew about my life and who I was. My one-night stand had a name. And that was Xander James. And Xander James was about to make everything in my life a whole lot more complicated.

Because Xander James was a lot more man than just being Mr. Tongue. Xander James was a man who took what he wanted when he wanted it, no questions asked. And now that he'd seen me again, I was at the top of his list of wants.

Read all of One Night Stand here.

ACKNOWLEDGMENTS

First off, I want to thank all of my readers for purchasing The Playboy. This book has come from my heart and I promise you that the sequel will be worth it. This book was inspired because I used to have a crush on Bradley Cooper and I always used to wonder what would happen if we ever met and had a connection. Unfortunately, that hasn't happened yet, so this book is all fiction.

I would like to thank my beta readers and newsletter readers that gave me feedback on the beginning of the book. Thanks go out to Sarah Milun, Krista, Kris Bihun, Kristen Whiting, Andrea Kohut, Rochelle West, Mary, Kim Lawson, Corie, Sharilyn Russell, Marcia Cowen, Kerri Long, Dana Vaughn, Danielle Forgione, Annette Dauzat, Jessica Hare, Kathy Shreve, Brit Conde Kayla Berry, Michelle Manfre, Leanne Butler, Terri Strudwick, Joanna Hollender, Jenn Allen, Donna, Joyce Black, and Sue Trotter. And if I was remiss and I forgot your name, please forgive me.

Huge thanks to Stacy Hahn, Vanna Rae-KB, and Kim Green for their help reading and providing proofreading feedback.

Thank you to my editor Sarah Barbour and as always my proofreader Marla Esposito. Your help is always appreciated!

Made in the USA
San Bernardino,
CA